*W*atch the Shadows

Watch the Shadows

Robin Winter

White Whisker Books
Los Angeles

ISBN: 978-0-9863265-0-9
Library of Congress Control Number: 2015933021

FIRST EDITION

Editor: Christopher Meeks
Associate Editor: Carol Fuchs
Book design by Deborah Daly

Published by White Whisker Books, Los Angeles, 2015

◆ I ◆

A semi thundered by, breaking wind like a fat man. Shorty Winsome hunched his shoulders before he slid sideways between two enormous eucalyptus trunks, down into the bark- and trash-filled gully, all kinds of crap getting into his shoes. Better no one saw him. The cops'd yank him off the highway, any excuse. Didn't like hoboes out here near the heavy traffic.

He preferred *hobo* to *vagrant* or *transient*. Made it sound like a choice. He'd had plenty of second chances. None took. He made his own way, and liked it.

Winsome followed a furrow behind the eucalyptus row, the sweat slicking the back of his neck. Going to be a warm day. California—best place in the world even if you're homeless. Even with the fleas. New York? Talk about the pits. Weather, grime, and crime, triple punishment. Couldn't get a decent night's sleep.

He patted his pockets, bulging with nuts and bolts, an almost new screwdriver, and a torn five-dollar bill. Shook his plastic shopping bag of flattened cans, then zigged to the left. Drawing those branches together had made a good hide.

He poked behind the brambles to locate his trash bag bulging with cans and bottles, and added his new take. A couple of bucks' worth. Bonanza. Oughta do this more often. Winsome dragged out his heavy backpack, propped it against a stump, and sat down, hunching butt-close to the pack before he hooked his arms in. Okay, time for the sweaty lugging. His stomach growled.

Patient down there, stomach. Today we have burgers at the MacDonald's, no crappy hand-outs from do-gooder Mrs. Meg at the Haven homeless handout in Isla Vista. She meant well, but sometimes a man needed a real hamburger, yellow cheese dripping, hot fries. His stomach rumbled.

◆ ◆ ◆

5

Winsome struck off in a straight line, angling toward a low spot in the fence, where wisteria dragged the highway fence down, making an easy clamber over. Now and again he took a sweeping glance around, making sure no one saw him. Being seen was a short cut to trouble.

Behind the string of shops and restaurants paralleling the freeway, he followed a new route, deep in the tangled overgrowth. The going was rough, but had one advantage. No one looking out the back door should see him, even if the bag of recyclables made him a big target. He smelled the waft of cigarette smoke from the service doors of one of the restaurants. A bramble snagged his cuff—he stopped. You could get thorns to let go if you were willing to back up. Then he saw it.

Black, sleek, gleaming like the sweep of a garbage bag, a shape melted through the bushes before him. The hair prickled on his nape. He saw the black plastic move as though a wind caught it, sweeping free of clutching branches, and flickering, slow, heavy. Made him think of an overfed bird. It passed under the road bridge a little further on, vanished.

Winsome whistled through his chipped front tooth. No wind, so what the fuck? Another semi-truck eddy? But he was too far from the highway, with its swooshing cars and groaning trucks.

He looked to where he'd first spotted the black shimmer and stared.

Meat? Something wrong about it, and then he realized: *no flies.*

Looked like meat. No skin. A shank piece. Pink, pale, pork, with streaks of fat and a little slick of blood where the end of a bone caught the morning light.

He didn't smell it. Must be real fresh. Wow. He imagined the scent of broiling pork on a spit over a fire. Pepper, salt and crisp fat. Where could he possibly make a fire today and not twig the cops? Bad thing about Southern California in fire season—all the worried eyes on scout for the rise of smoke, noses twitching for the stink of flames. He stepped forward.

Must've been tossed out, maybe dragged by a coyote that got scared off? He took a fast glance toward the restaurant, afraid that in his anticipation he might have revealed his presence to the smokers. "Vegan Paradise." Well, hey, this hank of flesh sure didn't come from that joyless place. No wonder they smoked, though he bet they did their best to keep the patrons and the boss from knowing. Smoking couldn't be vegan, could it?

He leaned in, sniffing again, afraid he'd pick up the tell-tale sweet stench of rot. Nothing but the slight whiff of blood and grease. God, he was hungry. He took a fast step forward, not minding the drag of brambles across his ankle.

He reached and grabbed before he saw the sneaker.

The Isla Vista Community Patrol,
October 7, 20xx
Vampire Attack? Gruesome Discovery in Isla Vista

Shorty Winsome, self-described hobo, found a dismembered leg on the side of Highway 101 in Isla Vista near the Embarcadero Exit Northbound. He told the Isla Vista Community Patrol that he may have seen a person unknown wearing a black leather garment or cloak disappearing under the Hollister road bridge near the scene of his discovery. The identity of the victim remains a mystery. Anyone with information is urged to call the Santa Barbara Isla Vista Police Force.

❖ **2** ❖

After midnight, Tuesday, a week into her high school sophomore year, Nicole stood barefoot on the warm flat roof over the kitchen, adjusting her telescope. Below her hummed unincorporated Isla Vista, university students roaming, music contending between speakers, parked cars crowding the sidewalks where there were sidewalks, the tinkle of glass in the cool night from someone's tossed beer bottle. Isla Vista vibrated, dense with people, most homes renovated to eateries or apartments, a community where the average age was twenty-something, the streets always threatening to break out into a public party. Nicole's parents wanted nothing better than this ferment of energy and enthusiasm, and Nicole loved living here. She'd never lived anywhere else. A drift of car exhaust mixed with the breeze from the ocean mere blocks away, so familiar, the heat of the day lingering in the grit under her toes.

Here was paradise on the coast, without governance, apparently without adults. Nicole, as a long-term resident, knew better, that the frat houses and overcrowded apartment buildings held a vigorous mix—surfers, scholars, dancers, college students, and professors, who never wanted to bottle the effervescence of this sun-toasted crowd. Rude and kind, the foolish and generous filled the streets, a chorus of homeless fringing the set. A mix of immigrants and poor combed the night streets for cans, bottles, or dumpster pickings. Noisy with parties, but with pockets of silence spreading away to the west, into suburbs with unfrequented streets and families who put up walls, grew hedges, and pretended their address was the next town over, never Isla Vista.

◆ ◆ ◆

Nicole waited for the Perseid meteor showers, due sometime from now until so long after bedtime that she knew she'd only stay awake for the opening salvo. She wished Dad were here, but if he were, Mom wouldn't have let her stay up so late. She worried about that. Dad not here, Mom not acting like herself; it was all like a tooth aching, not enough to talk about, almost an itch in the jaw that might go away if you didn't pay it too much attention. But it was like not thinking about the elephant.

Mom shouldn't to be willing to break the rules for her, Perseids or no. That was the elephant's trunk. Dad had never spent so much time traveling until this summer and fall. There flapped the ears. Nicole wanted to worry about her own stuff—friends, Denny Johnson, school, even college looming on the edge of next year—but family got in the way. A person heard so much about divorce, saw so much about it too. Now she could see the big bulk of the elephant, looming right here on the rooftop with her. She'd asked Mom if they were getting along all right, and Mom had looked startled, so either Mom was a good actress, or she hadn't a clue.

Parents often said things they couldn't possibly mean, but she was glad to see Mom shake her gray-streaked head and snort in amusement before saying, "We're fine. It's only this NASA panel your father got appointed to. I thought you'd be sympathetic to his having to spend so much time on it. Extraterrestrial life—what's not to like about a government panel looking into the possibilities for extraterrestrial life?"

Mom liked to repeat herself like that as if there were some

rhythm about her words that she always had to complete, as though she read from some zany script. "Your mom's weird," the other kids who met her said, and Nicole was kind of proud of that. Mom would never dye her hair or get her eyebrows plucked, or pretend she was a teen and wear Lycra spandex—that was for sure. Once, Nicole had seen her apply lip-gloss for the University Chancellor's Reception last spring.

"Does it look like I have lipstick on?" Mom had asked, and Nicole had said, "What good is it if it doesn't look like it's there?" which made Mom laugh.

When Nicole was younger, she'd sometimes wished her parents didn't stand out so much, stand up so much, put posters and political placards all over the yard, eat organic, and read or work all the time. She'd finally given up on them. It was OK. But this business of Dad having to travel every ten days had to end. Deliberately, Nicole closed her eyes and shoved that elephant off the roof. She looked around then to make sure, laughing at herself.

Hey, she caught movement out of the corner of her eye and swiveled to follow the motion. Meteor! Then she half-missed another. Forget the telescope—its field was too narrow. She'd only brought it up for company, anyway. Nicole sat down cross-legged on the still toasty roof, the dull glow of the University and Santa Barbara behind her so they wouldn't interfere, and hung her head back, way back, letting her eyes go out of focus. Ignore the sounds of someone climbing in the dumpster at the apartment building down the road, a rise and fall of voices—none of her business.

Breathe deep. Slow down. That was the best way to catch the flashes of streaking light. Holy crap, that was wonderful, a series of five, almost too fast to count.

Then a flaming streak of colors. Huge. She'd seen red or green or orange as a meteor burned up in the atmosphere before. But this one flared blue then purple, and seemed so near she ducked, her arms going up to protect her head. Did she hear it whine, or was it all in her mind?

"Shit!" Heart thumping, she watched it appear to plunge into the space between the sea and her house, maybe right onto the beach. She almost expected smoke or fire, but though she remained another few moments, her eyes straining in the same direction, she heard no sirens and saw no disturbance. Must have hit the sea or sand.

So much for wishing on stars; Nicole straightened her aching legs. She remembered too well the Tea Fire, the Zaca Fire, and the La Jesusita Fire. If she'd wished, it would be for no more fires, even if Dad said it was simply the price for living in a coastal desert with a fire-based ecosystem. Scientists for parents. How lucky could she be? Just wait until she got her high school science project going—no team for her this year; Nicole would work solo. Then Dad would let her use his equipment at the lab.

Something struck her wrong. Nicole stopped, sniffed, and shivered. An evil tang on the air, salty sweet, she didn't recognize it. Sniffed again, but perhaps only imagination misled her. She closed up the telescope stand and took everything in through the dormer window before going down the attic stairs.

"Nic? You're heading to bed? I meant to call you an hour ago."

"'S'okay," Nicole presented a cheek for her good-night kiss. "I did all my homework. I know you're busy with your paper."

Mom looked too awake for one in the morning. Her comfortable round face pulled into that not-so-comfortable expression it got whenever Mom was chasing an idea. Textbooks and journals piled on both sides of her, a stack of hand-scribbled notes under her hands, the familiar yellow lined sheets dented with the force of her writing—Mom did everything intensely.

"You have to teach class in the morning, too," Nicole said. "You need to go to bed now."

"In a bit," Mom said, obviously not really paying attention.

"That's what they all say. How many classes do you have tomorrow?" Mom didn't answer, lost already. Nicole shrugged and went off to get her shower. Parents. The moment you began to think you could take care of them was the beginning of disappointment.

3

Mr. and Mrs. James P. Addison. Brian, the postman, stood on the doorstep, balancing bulky packages and mail in his hands. He could hear Mrs. Addison inside, coming not so fast, to answer his ring. She opened the door clutching what must have been her husband's white bathrobe, blond hair pulled back from her made-up face, talking breathy on her cell.

Didn't the woman have a clue he had other Saturday deliveries to make? But he liked the bathrobe slipping off her shoulder. Wonder what that smooth tan cost her husband? Isla Vista had more fog than sunshine despite the shining image of southern California in the magazines he delivered.

Husband always spared a smile full of perfect teeth the days Brian came up the walk to hand deliver the mail because it didn't fit the skimpy lock box. No one else on the street bothered locking up their mail.

Brian could have been a robot, for all Mrs. Addison noticed. He'd arranged the letters, plus one that looked like it might be a check, on top of her mail, but did she seem to track?

Hey lady, I have a schedule. Not here for my health, even if my heart might get into overdrive if your bathrobe keeps answering gravity. Put down the freaking phone and take the bundle, unless you plan to give me an even better view… whew, that was close. Give my blood pressure a break—she didn't even start a blush.

Look at the polished nails. She held her fingers stiffly, careful, like she thought she could break those nails by one wrong touch. Who knew, maybe she could. Plastic? Wet with polish? She did smell chemical. Mrs. James P. Addison was damned pretty with her make-up on, but only styrofoam between those jeweled ears. Wearing nothing but earrings, now that was a picture.

He wasn't a man to her, in his gray-blue postal uniform and the navy cap. Hadn't she anything better to do than slither in her bathrobe gossiping on her phone at ten o'clock in the morning? She turned away already, not so much as a nod or a smile for his waiting, as cheery as if she chatted up a collection agency.

Next time he wouldn't bother to sort her mail, cards and letters on top, bills under, and then the scut stuff of flyers and magazines at the bottom for support. Let her see what kind of difference it made when she juggled that. Full frontal nudity was next on the program, dude.

But he'd get more embarrassed than she would. He had this thing about the mail. He'd rather run behind schedule than hand over a messy pile. Matter of pride. His job was the best—he chose delivery because he could do it the way he wanted. After the Army and the Gulf, that meant a lot.

The next house, however, had a *lady*, and some days he'd go all the way up the walk because it was raining, and he smelled cookies. Pretty, but in a way that meant coming home, her cheeks tired from smiling. No wonder, given all the years he'd been by, with her nursing her dad dying by the inch in the hospital bed in the front room.

Mrs. Meg Burdigal, husband five years gone to some secretary or bar chick. Fool. He left about a year before her dad died. A woman will care for her husband if she'll care like that for her dad. She worked half time at the Homeless Haven Center since her dad's passing, but Brian knew her schedule. The house always suggested baking, not nail polish or perfume.

She opened the door. He heard a man's voice in the background. Who was that? A deep, not unpleasant tone.

"I can smell danger, you know? There's an instinct to it. I tell you, danger's coming. There's a bad feeling in the air."

God, she looked happy, so happy you almost didn't see she buzzed with nerves. Dressed in neat brown pants and flowered blouse, Mrs. Meg had a glint in her eye that fitted the grin she gave Brian when he handed over her mail. Not that old, should have friends, but always bills on top for her. Nothing personal or nice. Brian sometimes cheated and put those invitation cards to get a manicure on top to soften the blow. He didn't think he'd ever given her good news in the mail, except maybe Christmas cards, but Mrs. Meg always had a smile to spare, and today—

"Here," she said. She must have seen him coming because she already had something in her hand. "Oatmeal cookie? Still warm."

"I'm allergic to oatmeal," Brian said and blushed. He never lied without turning red. His Josie used to laugh about it, said he couldn't even hide what he bought for her Christmas present. He could feel it. The red made him wish his beard went further up his jaw, that he'd left his hair down from its ponytail, but he looked over her shoulder and saw Dickhead sitting there on a stool at her kitchen counter.

No, not Dickhead her ex, but Dickhead the homeless man who put dogshit in his mailbag last week. Brian felt the blood come boiling up until he must have looked like cooked lobster. Felt like it. Dickhead appeared like a nice fellow too, just a bit down on his luck, clean with a good grin. Mrs. Meg wouldn't have seen the sly look in his eyes, the malice behind the rugged looks. What a sham.

Dickhead smiled at Brian, all his bigness hunched at the counter with oatmeal cookies and a glass of milk, *a glass of milk, goddamn it*, at his place. Looking tame, looking shaven, like she'd taken in a stray and given it a flea bath. Mrs. Meg, you don't have a clue.

"This is Dwayne Wallace, Brian, and I'm so sorry, I don't think I ever learned your last name?" She talked fast, always did.

The postman knows everyone, even the homeless, in a place like Isla Vista. They don't get mail, he's not responsible for delivering the post to them, but he sees them every day, talks with a few if he feels friendly, or recognizes the regulars.

Brian hated the way they made him feel. He tried to act pleasant, but *act* was the operative word. He knew a batch were vets like him, and that made him feel guilty, as if it were his business they couldn't get their shit together and get a job.

Worse yet, they didn't seem to hold it against him. What was he supposed to do, anyway? Let them sleep in his house and eat his food just because he'd been able to keep his brains in his bucket and pay his mortgage? Their problems were none of his business, and he didn't know how to clean his hand after having one of those high fives or a handshake pressed on him, without them seeing him do it. Dickhead had pretended to high-five him while reaching by with his other hand full of shit.

Being enemies with the homeless would be a hell of a lot easier. Nothing like a palmful of soft dogshit pushed into his bag to make him this loser's enemy. He shook his head at Mrs. Meg, wishing he could say something, and knowing by that smile on Dickhead's mouth sliding into a smirk, that there was nothing.

"Don't worry. Thanks though," he said and backed out onto the porch, trying not to see her embarrassment or the awkward movement of her hand with the cookie. No way did he want Dickhead to know his full name.

Where were her dogs, the smelly swirl of excited barking he usually faced when that door opened? Had she put them in the back yard for her guest? Bad news, Mrs. Meg. You should never put your dogs away for a man.

◆ ◆ ◆

Brian shook his head. Mrs. Meg probably invited Dwayne Wallace Dickhead in because he'd done some favor for her. Maybe helped her out with a dropped grocery bag. Brian tried imagining that, did he feel any better?

He felt uneasy, like he should go back and keep an eye on

things, make sure she was okay, that Dwayne wouldn't hurt her. He could picture himself breaking the glass on the front door, busting it open, and rushing in to throw that sucker out. Superman.

Yeah, sure, but Dwayne bulked bigger than he. Brian would probably fall on his face. Brian's smile hurt, thinking about it. Why smile? It wasn't so funny. Didn't Mrs. Meg know that men like Dwayne took advantage of women like her? Dwayne had that quarterback look, but any man watching him a while would know he wasn't a team player. He was the sort to target a good chance. Prey on the lonely. Sniff out the women with confidence thin as eggshells. Natural order of things.

Brian kept remembering the sensation of dog shit in his hand when he'd reached into his postbag, realizing too late exactly what that smell meant. Thank God it hadn't been too fresh, and that's a hell of a thing to thank God for. But squashy inside so he had to stop and clean every bit he could of the yellow smears off the top of the envelopes. Most got on the grocery flyers. He'd tossed them out though it made him feel like he'd broken a rule or something.

"—danger," what was Dogshit yammering about anyway? Danger came from folk like Dwayne; he should know all about it.

Another preferred stop here at the professors' house. Their kid was out under the apricot tree.

"Good day, Nic," he said. He knew that was what her mother called her. Cute girl, growing like a weed. Teen already. He found himself wiping memory of dogshit off his hand against his jacket before he reached in for the bundle. "Here's your mail."

"Thanks. You could simply put it in the box,. Why don't you?" she said, her pale face triangular, framed in black unbrushed hair. Too skinny for her own good.

"Because. Why don't you ever brush your hair?"

"I expect servants to do it for me," she said. "I'm waiting for my Nobel Prize and then my students will line up for the privilege."

Brian swept her a mock bow. Her dad gone again, the car out of the open garage. Something wrong there. No wonder she didn't feel like brushing her hair.

"Well, tell your boyfriend he's got a rival," Brian said, touching his cap.

It made her laugh. She spun on her heel and started back up the steps to the house with the mail.

"Hey," he said, on impulse. "Do you know Mrs. Meg? Meg Burdigal with all the dogs couple of doors down on Tarde Street?"

"Sure do. She used to teach Fiber Arts in my grade school. Quit to take care of her sick dad."

"She hanging out with anyone?"

"Nope. Why? Are you interested? She's one super lady," Nicole said. "Maybe a little religious."

"Hell, no," Brian said fast. "I'm a confirmed bachelor."

"Ha. You know the beginning to *Pride and Prejudice*?"

Unfortunately he did.

"No," he said.

"Liar," she said, cheerful and pleased with herself. "You're turning red. See you."

"Yeah," said Brian. Time to finish up. It was his day for putting his foot in it. That kid was too sharp for her own good. He wondered if her parents ever wanted to drown her. Probably.

Now she had him thinking about Josie again. Six years as good as marriage, he would have said, and then Josie took off. Two years and a half since, almost to the day. He still automatically noticed every anniversary—the first date, first sex, first fight, moving her in and toasting their new home with champagne. All the last days, too, and they filled a lot more of his memory than the good things.

God, no wonder he didn't want to go home. Maybe the place gave him those nightmares. Machines full of evil eyes, little feet pattering by his window. Was that something Freudian about Josie? Dwayne, more likely, with his chatter about danger.

Maybe he should sell. Clear out, start new. Next thing you knew he'd be sorting his deliveries and there'd be a big envelope with script on the front and a return address he didn't know. Envelope fat with an RSVP to Josie's wedding, as welcome as the extraction of his teeth. Yes, and a gall bladder removal. No, prostrate surgery—that was it. His mouth curdled with stale coffee. Allergic to oatmeal; what kind of line was that?

Another three streets to go before he could rest his aching feet. He shrugged his bag into a more comfortable position.

❖ **4** ❖

Another cool morning at the homeless breakfast service by the skinny wooden spire of St. Athos. Meg sat at the folding desk, checking the slips of paper in their envelopes, thinking about clean-up. Everyone fed, almost time to pick up the jars of peanut butter and of jelly. Hardly a crust of whole wheat bread left, three slices of the white. Meg knew a couple of people made extra PB&J sandwiches and hid them in their clothes. She looked the other way unless it was too big a grab; she hated to think of her folk hungry. She checked off the shopping list against the receipts.

Sudden movement erupted over by the big bench under the sycamore where Stu and two of his buddies sat talking in the foggy morning.

"Hey, Stu." Meg stood up, papers spilling from her lap. Stu looked like he'd been thrown right off the bench, sliding down onto the parched grass.

"Stu!"

He lurched on the ground, his hands flailed out.

"He's choking," Meg yelled loud as she could, hand fumbling for her phone.

"Choking man," she said to 911. "At St. Athos' breakfast tables corner of Pescado and Cortillo," She shoved the talking phone into her pocket, ran over, reviewing her Heimleich.

But he wasn't choking. He wasn't breathing. Heart? She put her head onto his smelly chest with weeks-old sweat and spilled food, and the raggedy scarf tickled her face.

"C'mon, Stu," she said. She yelled it, but no response, and God damn her—she hesitated before she pulled his head back. She finger-swept his mouth for anything in the way, missing teeth there—no dentures, okay for the breath of life.

Can't think about the taste of his mouth, can't.

She felt short of air; she had a hard time making hers push into his coffee and smoke-reeking mouth—felt to her like it just came back in her face. She remembered to pinch his nose, pull the jaw forward, then things went better.

Pump the chest, puff breath, try to keep count. She felt old now; there was no way she could keep up this pace; she had to slow down; where was Joe? Hadn't he been a paramedic in 'Nam? Or Karen, or anyone else to help her? Anyone from the staff? Anyone from the crowd? Stu felt so dead.

I'm not doing this right.

There's no one else.

I'm going to faint—I'm breathing too fast, breathing wrong.

Sure there wasn't a blockage in his throat? Sure he didn't choke? He was talking when this happened, not eating. She did another finger sweep of the mouth. Nothing. Then someone came running up, big and blue, put a hand on her shoulder, dropped to his knees and started the rhythm of chest thrusts, taking Stu from under her hands. Blue uniform, coverall.

Here came another, this one a woman, big boned and powerful with that ER technician clean-cut look. More ER guys full of quiet authority came, set down a gurney, bringing a bottle of oxygen with mouth-piece and a bulb. Meg slid back away on her butt, her eyes blurry with tears or panic or who knew what. Couldn't see anything anyway through those big ER techs bent over Stu.

◆ ◆ ◆

"I'm very sorry," the young woman said. Built like a Valkyrie, with short-cropped blond hair and a grave sweet smile. Perfect teeth, beautiful gray eyes deep with sympathy. "You did all you could. I just want you to know he couldn't have felt a thing. Maybe a massive heart attack, or aneurysm; they'll find out at the hospital. He may have died even before you started CPR. You knew him?"

"Yes," she said. Meg desperately wanted to brush her teeth, knew she looked ridiculous with the tears in her eyes. They came as fast and wet as though she'd been cutting onions, but all she could remember was Stu tipping his baseball cap to her that morning, when she hadn't had time for more than a nod and half a smile.

"Can you tell us his name?"

"Stu. Stewart Schaeffer. "

"Did you travel with him—do you know if he had family?"

"I'm not homeless," she said, more forcefully than she felt was right. Sloppy gray sweatshirt today—she should have dressed professionally. Damn it. "I'm the supervisor for the Haven Outreach morning breakfast. Meg Burdigal. It was cold, that's why..." shut up, Meg, it doesn't matter what you're wearing and why. "No, I think he mentioned a daughter, but he didn't tell us much."

Why had she said "us"? Did she mean everyone here, or was she trying to segregate herself from the men and women around her in their unwashed state, from herself and the staff at Saint Athos Church? Meg didn't know. She'd have to think about that later.

❖ 5 ❖

Nicole had worked on her science project four nights already. At school in the biology room, Mr. Marks began telling them *how*. The fluorescents shone off the top of his bald spot. He wanted them to work in teams, but she knew the way that would end. Other kids only messed things up and then expected her to finish the project and fix what they'd broken. Always happened the day before it was due, too.

This time she was going to stick to her guns. She needed a solo project. She'd learned some ways to be on better terms with her fellow students, but it wasn't easy. Didn't Marks see the best way to break the fragile friendships and acquaintanceships she'd crafted was him assigning her to work *with* some of them?

"Look, Nicole," Mr. Marks said, rubbing his forehead. He smelled of aftershave and mouthwash. First period in Sophomore Biology—she supposed it was better to meet him early in the day before the mint wore off.

The room was bleak with linoleum, long black tables, and flickering greenish light. Behind Mr. Marks's back someone was making faces at her. Denny Johnson, count on him to try and make her laugh when she shouldn't. She kept her face still and stiff. Whispering grew into little bursts of giggles and gossip. She wished she didn't notice how good Denny's smile looked. He winked at her.

"You have a lot to offer."

Blah, blah, blah. She thrust her hands into her pockets, squeezing her pencil stub.

Mr. Marks suggested, hinted, then ordered with all the bluster of an authority that had no confidence, his brown eyes blinking behind his specs.

"No, thank you." She wished she dared give Cyrano de Bergerac's speech that began with those words. But he'd think it was all sass. "I am *not* a team player. I do *not* work with my fellow students, and they do not work with me."

No contractions. She thought it sounded better that way. More decisive. He said some more stuff, but each sentence got weaker. The rest of the class settled behind him into a serious gab fest. Looked like Denny was telling a shaggy dog story that went on and on—

"Don't think I'll be easier on a one-woman show," he said at last.

"I don't. I fully expect the exact opposite," she said, her hands bunched in her pockets so he wouldn't see them shake. She hated confrontation, but she had to hold her ground.

He turned away and hollered the class to silence.

"You will have two months to bring your project to completion. I expect to see rough drafts, which will be 30 percent of your grade, by Thanksgiving. We are talking real laboratory work, real experimentation, real science here, folks. No exceptions."

Nicole had it planned. Polymerase Chain Reactions—she'd wanted to try PCR ever since her dad had shown her the machine in his lab, and she knew he'd let her. The idea of taking a piece of DNA and being able to "fingerprint" it the way they did in the detective work on TV was powerful. Hadn't she been hanging out at the lab forever? His grad students might help. She was always careful not to interrupt them or get in the way of work. She waited her turn even though it was her dad, and you might think she had some privileges.

PCR: amplify a couple of copies of DNA and familiarize herself with all the protocols. Maybe she could do forensic work for the police one day. It was a little common; all the kids wanted to get into forensics because of TV shows, so she bet her Dad would give her that knowing grin. But he'd still be proud she would take the time and finicky care to master a whole technique, a real scientist's skill. Maybe for the science project she could take some beetle or other and prove who its closest relative was.

Maybe she could prove that Denny Johnson was cousin to the cockroach. That made her smile. It's bad news when I smile, guys. You really don't want to work with me.

◆ 6 ◆

Late, she was so late. Ilene scowled at the mailman striding by. Wasn't his name Brian? Always looked like he had his shit together. Downright offensive to the rest of us. She pushed her grocery basket packed heavy with the sleeping bag and her boots, her clothes, saucepans, extra socks, and all her treasures, over the uneven ground, taking her time even though in the back of her mind she kept counting minutes. The Homeless Haven started serving ten minutes ago—if they had something special this Monday, it would go fast.

She had to get there, and if she hurried, she might upset her cart, and she knew she couldn't right it without help. Shaky this morning. Out of Vicodin for over a week, and booze didn't last as long as it used to, for killing her hip pain. No one to trust, not even the do-gooders at the Haven. What a stupid name—pretentious and promising what it couldn't deliver. Haven, as if they provided shelter. Only on really cold or rainy nights did they get the County to open the gym at the high school or the cafeteria at the diaper factory.

They oughta put bigger wheels on grocery carts. Ilene could hear her stomach gurgle, hungry. She wanted to cuss, but she felt rocky, a little weepy. Better not to waste her breath. She sure didn't want to get into another conversation at the Haven about old Stu having a heart attack or whatever it was the other day. The ambulance always came too late when it was for the homeless.

Usually Paul would have woken her in time to get going over to the church, but he'd been drunk last night. She'd left him in the coastal scrub, the idiot, snoring with his mouth so wide a duck could sit in it and crap. That would show him. Let him miss the handout in the morning—thin coffee and the makings of a peanut butter sandwich—unless someone brought oranges today. Seems they oughta do that more often instead of leaving the oranges to drop rotting off the trees around here. Rich bastids all. Didn't know the value of what they got, and screamed at you if you so much as took a single fallen fruit.

She stopped. A rat. Disgusting. She wiped the gray strands of sticky hair back from her eyes and looked again. Big pale rat, creeping around in full day. All swelled up; that rat must be really good at finding food. Or was it sick? She could report that to the

Haven folk; it would give her something more to say than thank you for your hand out.

Hand out of gag-worthy peanut butter. Never had liked peanut butter. Still she was hungry and her leg hurt something awful. Years ago, the doctor said she needed surgery, but dream on. Besides where could she keep her stuff safe while she was in the hospital?

Ilene squinched her eyes to get the rat in focus. Didn't look right. It seemed to move sideways like a crab. Legs bent wrong. God, that rat was Abby Normal. It was going to touch the wheel of her shopping cart if she didn't move on.

The animal lurched nearer. Blind? She couldn't see eyes in the pointy head. She pushed the cart at it. Scare it some. It stopped. There was the gleam of eyes. One, bluish and round like a fish eye, blinked at her from the shoulder. The other, slightly darker and clearer, focused on her from the furry chest.

Ilene swallowed hard against the acid that fouled her mouth. That was sick. That was wrong. Must be the drink she took last night. No more than a couple sips, but she'd needed it without the Vicodin, or she'd never have got a wink of sleep.

But the rat looked real. She veered the cart with a sudden burst of fear and made the concrete walkway, passing by a whisker. A whisker—that was a good one. She looked back once, pushing on as fast as she could. The rat still lay there on its side, the two eyes glinting with moisture in the weak sunlight. It moved again as though it wanted to follow her.

She had a sudden image of it slowly crawling through day and night to catch up with her, no matter where she found to sleep, down by the bridge on Hanks Avenue or up in the scrub off Camino Real near the airport.

No, she wasn't going to mention that rat to the Haveners. They'd know she was crazy.

◆ 7 ◆

Meg put out plastic knives, peanut butter jars, strawberry and grape jam, and bread—white, whole wheat, and a batch of day old rolls from Nancy's Bake Shop. Meg's breath puffed white in the cold morning air. With more time, she'd have made some of the sandwiches, but not today. She'd stopped at the Fry Donut Shop to get day-olds, and this morning they'd had seven boxes, about all she could juggle.

She hoped to see Dwayne Wallace, half-expected a big hand to close over hers and help her out with the pink cardboard boxes. She felt herself smiling and tamped it down with an apologetic word of prayer, thanking God for the day and the generosity of Nancy and the Donut Shop. Slow down, Meg. She nattered at God some days, hoped He didn't mind.

No, don't get to depending on anything.

She knew she was about as sexy as a tray of cookies, the past few years had taken brightness from her face and spring from her step. Maybe they would come back in time. Anyway it had been fun last week sharing teatime with a good-looking guy in her kitchen. She should make more time for friends. Dwayne must have had his check come in. She didn't know his schedule, she'd never asked, but he'd bathed, shaved, and cleaned up when she saw him that day.

He'd been on her corner sorting a collection of cans he'd picked up, maybe off the streets or out of one of the dumpsters. Nothing like students for dropping trash, even items of value, as though their parents never taught them to pick up after themselves. Student renters filled Isla Vista bungalows and low apartment buildings because of the proximity to the University, less than a half mile away. Always garbage on the streets here, bags blowing around. Little kids not yet in school came from many over-packed cheap rentals to climb in the dumpsters and pick out the good stuff for use or sale.

She smiled at four-year-old Bobby and his big sister Luanne. Donuts weren't nutritious, but what was life about if you couldn't have a nibble of sweetness every so often? She caught a shy glance from their mother, Amalie, so underweight, that one. Something more going on than met the eye. Meg's instincts made her worry about a wasting disease, AIDS, maybe an auto-immune disorder.

Health problems, some invisible until they struck. She wished she'd done more for Stu. Gone, and it looked today as though no one missed him.

"I've got a lead on housing for you three," she said to Amalie. "It won't be much, but it'll be better than the station wagon, and there'll be a pre-school."

"Thank you, Mrs. Burdigal." Amalie never met her eyes. She smiled at her shoulder as if she didn't believe what she'd been told, but appreciated the fantasy.

Meg heard a lot of complaining, especially from her church, about the homeless tracking litter all over the neighborhoods. Not her people. She knew these folk, watched how their numbers swelled when the economy shifted from bad to rotten. Felt a cold breeze on her own back when she saw again and again how few steps it took to default on a mortgage. No, the homeless she saw were all re-users, collectors, recyclers, not the source of trash.

She looked up fast when a big shadow fell across the end of the table—no, not Dwayne. She had to stop expecting him. He was only one of her people. She had so many.

Dwayne had told her some about his past, confided in her. No novelty there. A lot of the usual, an injury that took him out of work too long to hold his job down, a wife who thought she'd do better on her own once she gave up on Dwayne getting back to full-time work with a benefits package. Meg heard a lot of stories. Sometimes it made her anxious. Was she doing the right thing, holding this part-time job as Homeless Outreach Coordinator for St. Athos Church? No one could fix it all. She should prepare for her own future. Save a bit. Get a real job with benefits.

"Mrs. Meg," a woman said, whiney. Meg knew exactly who it was before she looked up.

"Ilene, good morning. We have doughnuts and rolls today," she said, infusing a warmth she had to pretend into her tone. "I hope you'll find something you like."

"It's nice of you to say so." Ilene ducked her head, the stringy gray hair falling across her face. "I don't like doughnuts, much. Sweets upset my stomach," Ilene scooped up two, slipped them into her sleeve. If she took one more, Meg would have to ask her to stop, suggest she ought to leave some for the others coming along in line, but Ilene always knew when she was on the edge, and turned away for her coffee.

The folk filed along, crowding up. Meg made small talk, asked how the night had been for a couple of her regulars.

"Something wrong in the park," a man she didn't recognize said to Charlie. "It eats the ducks."

"Mrs. Meg," Charlie said. He pushed a tiny old woman in front of him, her wide blueberry eyes worried. She stared at Meg. "I have Mrs. Fuller here, and she has a problem."

"May I help?" Meg said. "Please, Mrs. Fuller, take some breakfast."

"Mrs. Meg, do I have to pay?" The voice sounded thin, polite, and tremulous. How old was Mrs. Fuller? Meg had learned not to guess. Life on the streets kept its own timetable.

"Of course not," Meg smiled. "Never. We simply share what we've got and try not to run out before everyone's served."

"Mrs. Fuller needs a doctor," Charlie said, his weatherworn face important with information. "She got an infection in her foot, and it's gone stinky. Someone last week took her recyclables from her, so she's got no bus fare."

"After you've eaten breakfast, come see me, Mrs. Fuller," Meg said. "I'll make some calls." County Health, what a treat. She'd need to ask Jennifer to take over the office while she drove Mrs. Fuller the three miles there and waited for two hours, most likely.

But County Health would at least do something. Foot infections went bad fast, and you never knew if someone had untreated diabetes or circulation problems. Underlying conditions could lead to amputation following a simple infection. That was what happened to the Mexican guy who used to get about by bicycle—Tomas.

"Something wrong in the park," a long, tall man named Eric said. "It hums in the day. It hums in the night. The humming drives us mad."

"No, we don't need no help going nuts. It's all in your fucking crazy mind," a heavy-set smiling guy she knew as Winsome said.

"Crazy."

"Yeah, I said it," Winsome scratched his short colorless hair.

Where he'd gotten that name Meg couldn't imagine, unless it had been last year's assistant being funny. Or it was possible it was his real name, she supposed.

"Cool it, Winsome," she said. "You know how I feel."

"Yeah, about the fucking language," Winsome took the biggest of the remaining doughnuts. He made it sound like "language" had three syllables. "Sorry, Mrs. Meg. Sorry. It comes out of my mouth by accident."

He grinned, all his broken teeth displayed, and she nodded.

Where could Dwayne be? He hadn't told her he was leaving, and he was a regular. Maybe he had an appointment. Maybe he was trying for that job he talked about, cleaning corrals at the stables on campus. Could be anything. Meg hadn't seen him for maybe four days since the cookies and milk at her kitchen counter.

"The rats are going away." Meg didn't see who said that. "They know better."

She took a deep breath and regretted it. Hard for the folk without shelter to get clean, and it was toward the end of the month. She thought another apology to God. These were all His children. Moments like this made her doubt she was a good Christian. She shouldn't be able to smell them if she paid attention to the right things.

"Ten more days." Ginny said, wrapped in shawls and a long dress, the hem heavy with dried mud.

"Ten more days?"

"Till my monthly check comes in. My money. You know what I'm gonna do, Mrs. Meg?"

"Tell me," she said, even though she'd heard similar recitals for years.

"Get some vodka. Gonna check me into the Horizon Inn and take a two-hour bath. Add lots of new hot water every time it cools. All the soap and shampoo I want. Wash all my clothes at the Laundromat, order Chinese delivery from the Imperial Palace with extra eggrolls and spicy sauce, kung pao and rice, orange chicken to go with my vodka, turn on the movie channel and watch as long as I can keep my eyes peeled. Then it's gonna be Sunday. I'll go to the brunch at the Festival Restaurant on State and eat, starting on omelettes with cheese and salsa and hash browns and bacon and sausages…"

"Shut up, Ginny, you making my stomach hurt," Colin said, not altogether unfriendly in spite of the words. He scratched for the third time since he reached the table. "You ought to eat pancakes I say, with butter melting and syrup running all over the plate."

"Don't forget to buy your meds first," Meg couldn't help saying.

"Yeah, yeah, 'course I will," Ginny said and shuffled on. "What do you figure the vodka is?"

◆ 8 ◆

Brian believed he recognized the red Ford truck, so he walked faster to get by. He thought he knew the sort of thing that amused Mr. Dwayne Wallace Dickhead, and swinging the door out to hit him on the narrow sidewalk fit the profile. An old Ford Ram, once an expensive car, but with a couple of good dents and some baling wire keeping the bumper on. Red once, but patchy now, with the bed covered over by a homemade wooden cap. Did he hear snoring?

He took a deeper breath once he got past the cab, but something registered wrong. Brian turned, took a couple steps back. Why was he bothering?

Distorted face pressed against the glass. Dwayne leaned in the cab, his head crooked against the window, stubbled cheek making a pinky speckled flat shape against the fogged glass. Mouth gaping, eyes slit so just a little gray showed under the lids. Ugly as sin. Wish Mrs. Meg could see him looking like this. Not so handsome now. One big beached fish, looking drunk or sick.... Or sick. His breath clouded the windshield.

Brian hesitated. The longer he remained, the more likely someone would see him, would wonder what he was doing staring at a vagrant in a beat-up truck. Dwayne coughed then, a thready deep sound, hoarse. Made Brian's throat feel sore to hear. Damn it. He was an idiot.

"Mister Wallace," he called out. "Hey, there. You OK?"

Dwayne moved as if he wanted to respond but had trouble waking, trouble lifting his head from its bad angle against the window.

"You need some help?"

Hell, who was he to be offering anyone help? He didn't want to help. Wasn't his business. This was Dogshit Dickhead, remember.

Dwayne groaned, lurched against the back of his seat, more or less upright now.

"You drunk in there, or what?"

Sick or drunk enough to make no nevermind. God fucking damn it, why hadn't he walked on? Brian stood cussing himself for another couple seconds. Had to finish his deliveries, had to get someone to take care of this, but the only person he could think of was the last person Dickhead should have any contact with at all.

◆ ◆ ◆

"Mrs. Meg?"

Two of her dogs, the brindle shepherd and the black and tan mutt had already crowded between them. The black and tan seized his gloved hand in a friendly grip, shaking it like a toy. He let it enjoy, knowing it would let go in good time.

"Stop that, Popeye. Postman Brian?" Meg looked puzzled, buttoning her thick heathery sweater. Understandably puzzled. He'd never done a double delivery once in the seven years of covering this neighborhood. He never made mistakes. Popeye released his hand so he rumpled the dog's short soft ears.

"I'm sorry," he cleared his throat. "I know you work with the homeless folk around here."

"Yes?" She had the expression of someone who is expecting a complaint but doesn't yet know what to use as a defense. Did she find herself defending her charges a lot? Like the dogs' barking?

"The other day you had Dwayne Wallace here. Saw him in his truck a few streets off, a few minutes ago. Parked. He looks too sick to leave like that."

It was said. Did he imagine she reacted with more than standard concern? Mrs. Meg pulled the dogs back in, stepped out, and with a practiced kick to the door, closed them in with their barks of disappointment.

"Can you take me there?"

"Sure can. I'm still on my rounds, you know?" he hated the way his voice rose up like a teen's, making questions where none were needed. "We've had our run-ins," he said, wanting to slip in a warning about this man she befriended. "Dwayne and me, I mean."

"Do you know what's wrong?"

She walked faster than he, a welcome change from the few times he'd walked with other folk. People tended to saunter and that drove him nuts. Made his back hurt to walk slow.

Too anxious, she looked flustered. How far did this friendship go? They turned the corner, Meg in the lead. He wanted to put a hand on her arm, pull her back and go first, straighten Dwayne out a bit before she saw him. He saw Dwayne was out of the car, leaning on the hood. Not vomiting, was he—had Brian been wrong about that dreadful cough? Booze after all?

Then he heard it. More like a bark than a man's voice. He saw how Dwayne's arms sprawled over the hood for balance.

"God, he looks worse." His own voice surprised him. He pulled out his cell.

"I'm calling 911," he said to Meg's back. She reached to support Dwayne's sliding torso against the rusty hood. She pushed on Dwayne, and Brian stepped forward to assist. His other thumb pressed buttons.

◆ 9 ◆

Thank God for Postman Brian, medics and hospitals. Meg took a deep breath, made it a real prayer. She parked her little Miata at the curb under the tall Washingtonia palm. The glossy red car might be a post-divorce indulgence, but it made her feel good to handle all that responsive power under the little skate's hood. Second-hand bargain, but the little lovely car didn't look or feel like it. She adored a good engine. Maybe someday she'd take that course on engines at the city college and learn how to do repair.

Oh, who was she fooling? Last time she'd signed up was day before her dad called, sounding lost, to tell her about his doctor saying he had bone cancer. Maybe when she had a better idea of what came next in her life, she'd sell the Miata for charity. Poor thing. She put its bug-eyes down and climbed out, giving the sleek red side a pat.

Dwayne had double pneumonia, but the hospital put him on IV immediately for dehydration and added Cipro to the mix. No matter that they'd gone through a whole demeaning routine about treating him as if he had TB—Dwayne feverish enough that he didn't notice. Never mind how the hospital brought back bad thoughts about doctors and her dad gasping to death in his bed. You had to have faith in God, and sometimes even in doctors and hospitals, because some days there was no choice.

What? She stopped before her door, hand on the knob. The cat door jammed ajar? Odd, unpleasant. Looked like something slimy had been pulled through. Muck in the hinges. Had her fat tabby Schrand actually caught something, or dragged in a fish from the beach? She'd never known him to work that hard at anything; why would he start today? And oh dear, what a mess the dogs would make if Schrand brought in something dead.

Jelly-like slime, thick and gelatinous. Yuk. She opened the door and no dogs came rushing to greet her. Okay, if they were asleep, so much more a blessing. Thank you, God. She'd get her sponge mop and get as much as possible wiped up before they charged out. She slipped her shoes off as usual, and as usual, her slippers weren't waiting. Dogs always stole them.

Meg saw the viscid marks on her kitchen floor and paused a second to get a better angle on the reflective tracks.

They looked *wrong*. She was used to figuring out the traces various crabs or sea slugs and stranded fish made on the beach sands. Those told stories, often ending in a splay of feather impressions, bird tracks, the plunge of a beak.

But this… she couldn't figure. Well, it had been a long day, a startling day. She kept seeing Dwayne's fever-reddened face, his embarrassed attempt at a smile as if he thought she would judge him for the disarray and vulnerability of illness, the paunchiness of his face, while it simply made her feel protective. Bless Postman Brian for taking her to him.

The marks faded, drying. She got down on all fours, becoming aware of a sweetish putrid smell, rank. Only a little fishy. Funny, the smears had no resemblance to the straight drag she'd expect of Schrand with a fish. A lunging curving repeated track of indecision mixed on the linoleum with dirty dog prints.

She had to wash this floor anyway. Shouldn't ill-think the poor cat for having an adventure. Meg rocked back on her heels then stood. She didn't want that stuff on her socks.

She grabbed the blue sponge mop and wet it at the sink, following the trail of erratic goo, rinsing again and again. More than she'd expected. Where were the dogs? They should have heard her the first time she turned on the faucet. Where was the cat? The jellyfish itself, or whatever it was? Not in the living room—be merciful, Lord, she said, half-smiling at her presumption. As if God had time to save her carpets for her….

At the doorway to the living room, she stopped. Shocked, revolted. No jellyfish. This thing was unnatural, painfully wrong. Like the result of some experiment gone horribly evil. She'd heard what PETA said about the universities. They'd picketed the Biology Building on campus here for cruelty to animals.

It was a pulsating jelly with patches of fur, tabby fur, big glazing eye of blue staring back at her from the center. It blinked.

She screamed like a girl, throwing the sponge mop, and before the handle clattered to stillness was back out of the door in her stocking feet running for the family she blamed.

◆ **IO** ◆

"It's the University. Everyone knows they do experiments. Animal vivisection."

"Come again?" said Nicole. She'd never seen Meg Burdigal look like this, and it made her both uncomfortable and a little angry. Meg had always been cheerful and nice when teaching Fiber Arts. She'd brought homemade cookies to every class. Nicole looked down and stared at Meg's stockinged feet with bits of clinging grass all over the damp knit. Adults should act their age.

Nicole had been in the middle of her French homework—difficult enough to make herself start. Now she'd have to start it twice.

"I'm sorry, Nicole. I should talk to your dad, perhaps."

"Why?" said Nicole. That came out harder and faster than she'd meant.

"Isn't he home? It must be time for dinner."

"We eat late." Dad being gone was none of Mrs. Meg Burdigal's business. "He works late."

"Not that late," Mom said. Nicole jumped. She hadn't heard her mother come up behind her.

"He's away. You said 'some problem at the University'?" Mom said.

"No, in my kitchen."

Nicole stepped back. Mom could handle Meg, even if she'd gone whacko. Mom could handle anything.

"Come on in. Meg, is it? Or do you prefer Mrs. Burdigal?"

"I'd prefer the University stopped experimentation on poor helpless animals," Meg said. Wow, rude. Nicole saw her mother straighten up, stop in her half-gesture of invitation.

"In your kitchen?" Mom said. "Experimentation?"

"Your laboratories made it. One of those wicked vivisection

labs. There's no other explanation—nothing that looks like that could be natural."

Meg's voice wobbled, and Mom put out a comforting hand. So Mom didn't think Meg crazy? Something else was going on?

"Come sit down and tell me about it."

Nicole didn't wait for an invitation to join them. She planted herself on the end of the couch and watched Meg grasp the offered glass of water as if to anchor herself in space and time.

The story of her kitchen slime animal had Mom nodding, but speaking little. Nicole interrupted.

"So what makes you so sure it isn't some sea creature your dog dragged in and chewed? You know jellyfish eat fish and there could be a fish eye tangled up in…?"

"No. It wasn't like that. It isn't a creature God ever meant. It had fur too. Stripy fur like my cat."

"Let's all go and see," Mom said. "I'm sure there's no getting any homework done until we settle this. But Mrs. Burdigal, I can assure you that we microbiologists don't create life."

"No. Only God can do that," Meg got to her feet. "But do you violate scripture by combining forms of life? I've heard stories."

"So far as I know, and I do work in one of the largest laboratories on campus…" Mom began.

"No, she doesn't just work there, she runs it. It's her lab." Nicole had to put that in. Meg should know whom she was interrupting and throwing absurd accusations at.

"There's no chimeric work going on in any of our laboratories, and we are not violating any scripture."

"If you even know what scripture says," Meg said. She said it low and she probably didn't mean to be heard.

"Mrs. Burdigal." Now Mom's voice had a degree of frost. She closed the front door and started down the street with Nicole on her heels. "I studied like a good Christian with the Jehovah's Witnesses for three years, and I suspect my knowledge of scripture would stand up to yours."

Nicole almost stopped in shock. She stared at Mom's comfortable round face and her blunt nose, her mouth usually smiling but now straight with warning. She'd never heard Mom tell anything like that before. Jehovah's Witnesses—Jehovah's Witless, as she and her companions called them. No, Mom? Never. Mom going door to door with *Awake!* magazines in her hand? Mom choosing to knuckle under to any authority she promised not to question? But Mom never lied. Nicole looked at her mother's neat head bent in thought and Mom seemed part stranger. If that were true, what else did Nicole not know about her own parents?

They walked out, down the street, the fine evening coloring up the sky with turquoise. Yes, Nicole remembered this was Meg's house with its Washingtonia palm at the end of the driveway.

They turned under the palm tree, and went into the oddly silent house. Nicole walked straight for what appeared to be the living room before Mom or Meg. Smelly. She refused fear. She was a scientist. There was the mop on the floor, but no creature.

"It's crawled away," Meg said, twitchy fear in her voice. "Where's it gone? Is it hiding?"

Nicole got down on all fours and Mom did too, looking for clues. It was too creepy for words if Meg's creature had slithered away to hide under the furniture. There were no traces except the big sopping circle where Meg said the thing had lain. Like someone left a jelly to melt there, aspic maybe, with no scent of fruit, only a rotten stench on the carpet.

"It's gone," Mom said, "but where are your dogs?"

Meg looked so upset now that Nicole rose and put an awkward arm about her shoulders—gave her a quick hug. Embarrassing.

"Let's look for them," Nicole said. "Were they in the house or the back yard?"

"I left them in the house and my roommates haven't come back from work yet to let them into the yard. I rent–two great students share my house…" Meg's voice jittered.

Hesitating in the corridor of the small house, Nicole heard a tiny whimper.

They found both dogs under Meg's bed. Nicole couldn't believe that the boisterous duo refused her offered hand. Meg did serious coaxing to get them out—wriggling doggy-smelling beasts who had no interest in returning to either living room or kitchen.

◆ ◆ ◆

"Do you believe Mrs. Burdigal?"

"I think you're old enough to call her Meg now. She told you it was OK," Mom said.

"You're avoiding the question, Mom," Nicole said.

"I am. I don't know how to answer responsibly. I can believe she saw something unusual, but it's likely that if we'd seen it, we would have been able to figure it out. She's no biologist."

"No," Nicole said. "That's for sure. Mom?"

"Yes?"

"You never told me you were religious once upon a time."

"I still am."

"What?"

"I'm still a believer in God," Mom said. "But I don't believe in telling other people how to believe or why."

"Even me?"

"I never knew what to do about that," Mom said. "I didn't want to brainwash you."

"So do you miss the Jehovah's Witnesses?"

"God, no," Mom said. "I feel that if God gave me anything, He gave me freedom, beyond the rules of man or the desire of religious men for power over their fellows."

Nicole tucked her cold hands around Mom's warm arm and leaned against her. Awkward to walk, leaning that way, but it felt good.

"We should make something for dinner when we get back," Mom said. "It's later than I knew."

Nicole felt the wet in her pocket slowly leaking through. She didn't have to tell Mom about that, not yet. One little patch of the tabby fur that she'd pulled off the carpet from that gooey area. Nicole shuddered—gross. A scientist should never think *gross*. Guess she needed some practice. She'd never go anywhere again without a zip-loc baggie in her pocket. She was going to change these jeans and get them into the wash as soon as she could.

"You're cold. Chilly in the shadows when dark falls these days. I don't recall the cold coming so early last year," Mom said. "By the way, I forgot to tell you I may ask you to do me a favor. A friend of mine's moving in to town this week. She has a son your age and I think he might end up at your school Be friendly, will you? I like his mom a lot. We go all the way back to grad school."

◆ **II** ◆

Brian wasn't hungry yet even though it had come on full dark. Too soon in September, the days pinched down. But Brian wasn't about to want anything but a quiet time, a cup of soup, and a muffin with cheese. Josie had liked parties, dances, going out to hear music. Stop. No more remembering things he coulda woulda shoulda done, just the job ma'am, just the facts, just a little time in the evening with a joint and a drink after his dinner, and no one bugging him for more or better. Time was, he would have said he was good in bed, but Josie had taken that with her, too.

But it wasn't true. He still wanted women, yet having one was so complicated. You had to talk, relate, and as soon as that happened up popped a quadrillion ways to go wrong and not even know what was happening until too late.

Friends—that would be nice, but everyone dropped him when Josie left. Maybe they always were more her friends than his, though he wondered sometimes if divorce and partings and death made people avoid you because they saw the potential of an end for their own partnerships in your face. "Let's get together sometime" had got to be the most repeated lie he'd ever heard. A lot of them had kids too; that kept them busy. Or had he missed the train, the plane, the bus, and the horse and all—those kids were already grown, on dates, in high school or even college? Look at Nic, next thing you knew she'd be getting a scholarship to some Ivy League snot factory, and she'd never joke with him again.

Hard to tell when you had no kids of your own. Not that he regretted, oh no. He'd have been an awful dad. Too selfish. You only had to ask Josie.

Brian sat down on the sofa and looked at the dead face of the TV. He really didn't feel like watching football or basketball or the news. What else was there? He looked around the room painted in pleasant almond. The few items of furniture that Josie hadn't wanted made it look bigger than it was. He should furnish the place properly. Should buy some books, more comfortable chairs. Upon a time he'd liked to read, liked to read about railroads and wild country and maps. But why bother? Who could sit in more than one chair at once anyhow?

Only a thousand channels and he'd bet not a single one he wanted to see. He would get a beer and some nuts—maybe that would make something on the tube more appealing. He pressed the on button and began to flash through channels, stopping and going back a click. That guy looked like him without a beard, his mouth looser than Brian's, but not a bad mouth. He touched his own as if touching it could reassure him that it was still his own, still under good control, and made himself smile at his foolishness, though it tasted sour. The guy in the movie looked a little over-dressed to be hanging in a Starbucks, and you could see the love-ly heroine giving him the eye, tossing her dark hair in a swirl over her shoulders to catch his attention, the soft fabric pulling across her breasts, then pretending she hadn't noticed anyone watching.

You look at the guy in Starbucks, at the way he's chosen his clothes with care to present a good image to the world. You see his face, attractive, a set of features that suggest a story, eyes to match. Looks employed, looks fit, has a world of thought in his dark eyes, and what you don't see, what you don't know, is he's barely there at all, hardly held together with masking tape and paste. Chewing gum and baling wire. Whatever. He's scarcely one whole thing. He's taking up that cup of French Roast and sipping it, hot as it comes, to remind him he has a throat, but you, girl, see only that single guy with a laptop leaning up to the counter. What's in his eyes is the washed up grounds of bad dreams.

Brian aimed the remote, clicked off the TV before he could sec-ond-guess himself and change channels instead. The emptiness of the room held him in its hand. Maybe he needed a dog. Or even a cat. If he weren't a postman, he could go take a walk. Big career mistake to take a job that kept him active all day, so there wasn't much point to getting some more exercise at night when he could-n't settle down. He turned off the living room light, went to the park-side window, pulling up the rice paper blind. Josie had cho-sen that. Pretty dusty now. If she were here, she would probably have had it cleaned or something. He stared out into the blue night, his sight adjusting to the dark.

Benches, trees, the rising toss of bushes, the sequence of palm trees. He'd been in high school during the Isla Vista riots, but he'd missed the day they burned the bank. Busy studying chemistry. Now they'd named the spot across the road from the bank Freedom Park. Here, next door was a cheap house even as Isla Vista prices went, because lots of folk didn't like the idea of a house right next to a park full of homeless. He'd trade up one day.

He squinted. There was some kind of movement out there.

First thing he thought of was water, perhaps, maybe a leak in the park's watering system. The grass moved, not the kind of movement that meant wind. His breath clouded the glass—he thought *damn*, backing off and wiping it down, holding his breath this time.

The grass glowed softly in the park, all of it oddly illumined. Maybe an effect of the fluorescent streetlight. The grass sent out what appeared to be little flat tendrils, waving like eager tentacles of a sea creature. Made him think of sea anemones. He felt cold, the hair on the back of his neck standing up like this was a movie. Brian stared until his eyeballs ached. If he went around to the door, would it be gone by the time he could go out and put a flashlight on it? The grass rippled now, like a shaken carpet, the waves seeming to give the entire flat of grass a movement toward the street. It flowed, purposefully.

He felt himself clench his teeth. He pushed back from the window. Hadn't even smoked a joint tonight or had anything strong to drink. He had to go see this thing. If there were miracles, they didn't have to be bad miracles. Mrs. Meg believed that. He'd always thought the opposite, but if the grass had come alive in a whole new way, who knew what was possible?

"What's possible, God?" he said out loud, as if he thought this once God might answer. But God hadn't answered in the dust of war. Why would He bother now?

Brian grabbed the flashlight, flicked it on, swore. Batteries dead. He didn't dare turn the lights all on in the kitchen, settled for the one over the sink. He stuffed fresh batteries into his yellow plastic flashlight. Yes, that worked. He shut it off then went for the side door.

Outside, there was no significant wind, only the usual Isla Vista smells of ripe garbage, a faint whiff of beer, the overriding scent of the briny sea. Music thudded in some house off the main drag to the west where the fraternities clustered. Brian waited again for his eyes to adjust, then moved around the corner of the house, flash ready in his hand. He pushed through the low hibiscus bushes on the side of the park then stopped. Nothing. Nothing strange, anyway. The grass didn't seem particularly bright— looked the way it always did, trodden, dry, sad. Brian turned slowly, extending all his senses for anything that seemed out of the ordinary.

A vagrant dog, small and skinny enough to look un-owned, moved slowly down the paved part of the street. Brian thought it knew he was there because it had a slight cant to its head with a sideways fashion of trotting along. If he were a good citizen, he'd catch it. Poor pup looked starved, flea-ridden no doubt. Did he have something good to eat he could use to lure it in? Brian cast one more wary look about the street and yet again at the park, but there was nothing that resembled the sea anemone movement he'd seen earlier.

Bit of hamburger, then the pup would probably come to him. He had some rope soft enough he thought he could collar and lead it. Idiot. He'd probably get bitten. He knew better than to tackle even a small dog. He didn't want to have to get rabies shots, did he? Even as he envisioned every bad outcome he could imagine, he went back outside, glancing about. But the dog was gone. He walked up and down, whistling a small hopeful whistle, but there was no dog. Just the usual bits of trodden garbage, a runnel from someone's dropped Coke here, there a swathe of slime by the drain in the street.

Brian looked round again, sharp disappointment erasing all the stranger feelings about what he thought he'd seen moving along the ground in the park. Illusion. Some odd refraction of the window glass. No unusual glow. Maybe he'd seen a fragmented reflection. He'd go in, check it again.

A few minutes later, standing at the window, Brian tried tilting his head in various directions, but he couldn't replicate the weird impression he'd had of moving grass. The more he tried to recall exactly what he'd seen, the less likely it seemed—the more he doubted his own memory. There was that little dog again. He looked at it nosing about, but he suddenly felt too tired to worry about it anymore. The impulse was spent. He closed the blind. Maybe tomorrow, if he saw the pup, he'd call County Animal Control.

◆ ◆ ◆

The door opened, the rattling bark of dogs announcing Brian as if they were paparazzi exposing a scandalous secret. All the lights were on inside this overcast day. Smell of dogs and bread baking, maybe something like stew in the pleasantly steamy room. He had the impression of sparkling cleanliness of floor and counters in the kitchen.

Mrs. Meg was in an apron, Mexican appliqué making a splash

of hibiscus on her front with a fantastic bird flying toward her shoulder. She smiled. Maybe he would tell her about the dog he'd seen.

"Mrs. Meg, here's your mail," Brian said. He handed over the stack, bills on top. Her bounding dogs almost knocked the lot from his hands, but he grabbed in time.

Popeye circled, bumped hard against his knees looking for a go at his hand. Brian didn't feel like it, ignored all that friendliness he hadn't earned. Maybe he wouldn't tell her about the pup.

"Thank you," she said, and there was a glow on her. Meg seemed cozy in her soft lavender jumper with fantastic apron. She looked pleased, lively, interested and full of anticipation.

"Brian?"

"Yes?"

"I'm missing my cat. Don't know if you know Schrand, big fluffy tabby with an enormous tail. Maybe a little overweight."

"Of course I know Schrand."

Schrand took to the streets after Mrs. Meg fostered the dogs from some homeless guys who ended up in prison a couple years back. Schrand hadn't approved of the dog invasion, but he only got fatter, so Brian hadn't felt too sorry for him.

"I'll keep an eye out for sure, Mrs. Meg. How's the patient?" he made himself ask, but he thought he knew the answer. Dwayne's red truck was slouched up to the curb at the end of her driveway where it blocked the view of anyone trying to pull out.

"Much better, Brian, and thank you so much for what you did. Bless you. You know they tossed him out of the hospital as soon as they could disconnect the IV? He couldn't go on sleeping in that drafty truck, so I made him up a bed in my garage. The doctor says it can take twelve months before the lung scar tissue from pneumonia heals."

"Oh, so that's why you're parking on the street."

"Yes," she said.

"Providing refuge," he said. "Be careful Mrs. Meg. There's always more to a man than his first story."

"That's dear of you, but you can mind your own business," she said, a smile taking the edge off it. "I'll take the guidance I'm given. Maybe there are many ways of following Providence?"

"Could be," Brian said. "I'm out of practice on following, myself."

He didn't have PTSD. They'd tested him for it. He didn't want to do any following, ever again. Brian was half way down the path to the street when he realized he'd turned away from her without a good bye of any sort. He glanced back over his shoulder, but she'd already closed the door, the eagerness of dogs stilled. How many feet from the garage to her bedroom? Mrs. Meg, you haven't a clue what it is you do. Hope to heck your God does.

◆ 12 ◆

"Sure they had me on some drugs," Dwayne said, shrugging, as though to relegate the idea to its proper, lesser importance. He gave her one of those wonderful intimate smiles where half his mouth slid up as though making fun of himself. He looked so much better, the color back in his face, the creases in his lean cheeks emphasizing his humor. "I only go natural these days. Organic, healthy stuff. Need to watch what you put in your body. All those chemicals and poisons can build up inside. I like home-opathy and all that."

"And wine," she said. He gave her a fast look that set her back in her chair. Then she reached for his arm and touched the flannel sleeve. Her husband's old blue plaid looked great on Dwayne with his deep-set eyes and silvering brown hair.

"I was joking," she said.

"That's OK, then," Dwayne said. "Been times in the past peo-ple rode me all the time, and it makes me jumpy to feel folk being critical. Taking notes on everything. Once burned, you know?"

"Wine's natural," Meg said. "Our Lord drank wine."

"Even made wine," Dwayne said, and that cheered her.

"Yes," she said. "The wedding at Cana."

"I went to church upon a time, when I was little—out in Ohio before I signed up for Basic."

"I didn't know you went to the Army," she said. It troubled her how many veterans hit the streets.

"Chose not to stay, but it's a black mark on my record. Discharged for losing my temper a few too many times. That's why the meds I mentioned. But I sure don't need them now. Hey, can I fix that kitchen sink? Would you mind? If you've got some washers and a wrench, I can take care of that drip and maybe empty the trap while I'm at it. Would that be OK?"

◆ 13 ◆

In the brightly lit laboratory, Nicole put her first batch into the PCR machine and closed the red and white hatch, only letting out her breath when she heard the latch snap. Her hands felt sweaty in their latex gloves. Sam, looming in his white lab coat, nodded, his brown ponytail bobbing.

"Perfect protocol," he said.

He was one of Dad's grad students, and she would have thought he was cute if he hadn't been so much older and almost part of the family. All grad students acted like her older siblings, which could have been frustrating if she'd been like other girls. But she wasn't. She didn't want to have a guy underfoot until maybe after college.

"What's your sample from?" he asked, turning away as if going back to his own work.

"Just a piece of a friend's animal."

"Animal?" he said. "That's an odd way to put it. What is it, an anteater or a wombat?"

Nicole laughed and liked the way his big mouth smiled. God, if she could just get him to show up once at school, that would get the gossipers going. Tall, skinny, and so sure of himself. While envious voices might call him a geek, everyone would know she had outdone them all. Outclassed them all. Even Denny Johnson. But, too bad. Sam was family. She had to keep thinking that way. She knew the house rules. Mom and Dad were so clear. No embarrassing the grad students by flirting with them. No blushing, no crushing.

"A pet, I should have said." She made up her story on the fly. Why she didn't want to explain about Mrs. Meg's weird puddle of animal goo on the floor, she couldn't rationalize, even to herself.

You're a bad liar, Nicole; make it short. "A cat, I think, but they were challenging me, so I don't really know for sure. Might even be someone's snake."

"Well, you realize this isn't a random identifier," Sam said.

"Yes, I do," she stripped off her own lab coat and hung it on the rack. But if there were something unusual about Mrs. Meg's scare, she hoped the sequencing might show it up. "I am my father's daughter, after all. All I have to do is say if it's a mammal."

Nicole went down to the bookstore on Sabado Street and buried herself for the next hour there, paging through the science fiction section. Lovecraft—hadn't her mother recommended that? But the language was so old-fashioned. She read on, and after a few smiles at the archaic voice, the story itself swept her in. She found a spot to sit down.

"You're bending the covers," a voice said. "I could tell on you."

Nicole jumped, looked up. Did she know this man? He coughed, a hoarse deep cough, and she thought she smelled something rank on his breath. A big guy with slightly stooped shoulders, as though he wanted to look smaller or younger than he was inside his greatcoat. Smooth shaven. She'd seen him before; yes, she had. One of the homeless ladies had been throwing some stones at him as if she were really mad.

Nicole stood up and stepped back, angry, but decided that not answering him was her best choice. She knew how to treat a book, and she'd decided before she sat to read that she was going to buy this one.

"Princess, you're an arrogant bitch; that's what's wrong with you. Had your way paid all your life, I bet. It won't be like that forever. Things happen—even to the best of us."

He continued talking after her as she strode toward the cash register.

Mr. Gorham took a moment to realize she was waiting, and Nicole fidgeted, not wanting the big man in the back of the store to follow her. It was growing dark outside, and she knew she was expected at home.

"Oh, Nicole," he said, and Nicole wished he hadn't said her name in case the man was listening. "Is this all for you tonight? Better get yourself along home. Your dad still off in DC?"

"No," she lied. She liked Mr. Gorham, but he had no business tattling her private life in public like that. In the dull glow of the green shaded desk lamp, he looked like a skinny gnome from a children's book as he counted her change. She assumed he'd never get a cash register. He always figured everything down to the last fraction of tax on a pad of paper with a gnawed pencil stub.

"You win on the tax today, young Nicole. Comes out to .344. Bingo."

He always joked like that. Nicole thanked him and checked back over her shoulder, but she couldn't see the big man. Maybe he was looking over the back shelves. Nicole ducked out the door and ran the first three blocks, cutting, after that, across the corner of the park. Slowing down, she felt much better. That was probably the sort of guy her mother would have told her to counter-aggress. Some people needed to be swatted back, or they would keep leaning in on you. But it was hard to tell sometimes, and she hadn't wanted to engage with him in any way. It was a choice. This part of the street was better lit, and she slowed down even more, patting her book.

But it was gone.

"No; oh shit," she said out loud and the sound of her own voice surprised her. She looked back down the street. Twilight and past. Mom might not notice if she were late. She thought about leaving the book lost, and the idea hurt. Silly though it seemed, she felt as if the book would miss her, feel deserted. Dropped in some gutter with the stale beer and coke cans, meaning nothing to anyone but her.

She began to retrace her way.

"Shit shit shit shit shit," she said, and the word soothed her with repetition. She kept imagining she saw the flutter of pages just there, under the bush, or no, over in the shadow of the verge by the Volkswagen with rust spots. She'd spent her own good money on that paperback right down to the tax. She wasn't going to let it lie abandoned somewhere in the street. She jogged through the park, straining her eyes, then let herself walk again. That's what you got for being a nerd. If she were a track star, she wouldn't run out of breath this easy.

Two blocks from the bookstore on Sabado, she saw it, and she swallowed in relief. Right smack in the middle of the pavement. She was so focused on it that, when another shape bent down and another hand reached for it, she almost blurted thank you.

It was the big man from the back of the bookstore. He was holding his coat closed with one hand, awkwardly, and her first thought was—he's a flasher. I can scream for Mr. Gorham, but he's probably reading.

"Someone lost her book," the big man said. He looked like all the bullies she had ever seen coming up through school. He had that expression with the eyes narrowed in anticipation, dandling the book as if to tempt her to snatch it back. He laughed, and she wanted to hit him.

Be smart, Nicole; getting involved with this guy isn't worth it. You know that, don't you?

Then two things happened. A sound came from Mr. Gorham's shop, probably nothing more than a dropped book, but it made the big man jerk, and when he did a magazine fell out of his coat. Without a plan, Nicole leapt forward, swept the book from his fingers, and was off in a start that would have done the track coach credit. She had never run so fast. She heard a shuffle, felt the movement of air as if he grabbed after her, but Nicole knew better than to hesitate. Or look back.

No footsteps running after her, no swearing, simply silence. She ran all the way home, stopping only when she stumbled onto the front steps of the house. Alarm sent her hands to patting—cell phone, yes—why hadn't she used it? Wallet, OK. Keys, present. Book. Yeah, book. She looked at the battered cover with love. *The Best of H. P. Lovecraft*, edited by August Derleth.

◆ 14 ◆

Still stewing over the incident by the bookstore this evening, Dwayne poked around the garage. That snippet of a black-haired girl with her book, arrogant, as he'd told her—spoiled. He could have told her a lot more home truths. Time someone kicked her into line. Little piece of sass. Too bad she'd gotten away. Would have been fun to give her a good scare—teach her something about the real world, break her out of her snottiness. He'd been too short of breath. Mrs. Meg said it took a year to heal the deep damage pneumonia did.

Meg had told Dwayne, apologetically, that she wanted four shelves in the garage. At least she treated him with proper respect. Right here, along the west wall of the garage, with maybe two-foot depth, bracing, and a head room of eighteen inches between shelves. Top open for the light stuff, like the bags of styrofoam peanuts and empty cardboard boxes.

Dwayne fiddled with the boards she'd bought and thought about planning the cuts. But he felt too comfortable, too relaxed to focus. He sat down on his blue-and-green-quilted bed, made of stacked mattresses Meg and her roommates had dragged out here for him. Not a pretty place here in the garage, but out of the world. Out of the way.

That was a nice dinner last night; Meg had given him a nice place to land, though some of the time he wasn't quite sure where he stood with her. He ought to find out. A good woman, kind of cute. She could be a lot more.

He looked at the aluminum L-braces. Easy assemblage, even if she had shit for a drill, one of those lightweight woman's Sears doohickies. What if he fancied those shelves up a bit? Impressed her? Wood all around, reinforcements, and a batch of screws twice the length of what she'd bought?

He could get used to it here. But who was he fooling? He'd had good places before, a good woman, a good bed, a good territory. Good didn't cut it. Good never did. He'd probably eat his way through and get tired. Empty the shell, toss it away, and move on.

Still, maybe he could take some time. He needed to get his lungs healed before he hit the road. He had a chance here. Meg was religious, that could make things interesting. He liked challenges. He could settle in for a real rest here; he might even marry Meg if he liked. A man came to an age when stability meant something. Move the roommates out. Didn't like the way they looked at him anyhow. Stay a couple years. Nothing like having a house and a cook and, even if Meg wasn't young or hot, she was comfortable. Cute even. Looked giving, in the right way.

But she'd bore him. Yes, that was a thing. He couldn't stand boredom. He wasn't a settler for less than the best. Not for the long haul. No. Good didn't cut it. Never did. Yet a bit of profit, a bit of rest, a woman once divorced could be way easier to gentle than one who'd never married. She knew how to let go, how to share, or she wouldn't be here living this life. She liked to take care of people; well, why not him?

He was good himself; she'd be lucky to have him. She ought to be grateful. She would be. Take her soft. He'd be nice to her. He knew what she'd like.

◆ 15 ◆

"Meg, do you have a moment? May we talk?"

The rising breeze shifted a chilly morning fog around the church. Meg turned from the church steps to see Karen Codrall, her strawberry blond hair blowing across her elfin face, her children clinging, one to each hand. Another on the way, God bless them.

"Of course," Meg said. "Sure, Karen, you mean now?" She rubbed her hands together, wanting something to do with them. Karen always set her off balance. She never felt at ease with Karen and John, they seemed so perfect.

Karen turned and signaled with her head to her handsome husband who courteously broke off his conversation with Father Stephens and loped over. Remarkable to see a man so responsive to his wife, unusual for Karen and John, in specific. What was up? Karen usually waited on John. John took both toddlers by the hands, and with a greeting nod to Meg, aimed the kids away towards the park.

"I wanted to ask you for an honest answer about something that's been troubling me," said Karen. "Let's walk this way, shall we, so no one else has to hear?"

What kind of trouble could this devout young couple have? Meg appreciated Karen's company at the church in various projects and Bible study discussions even if sometimes she believed that Karen interpreted the role of women in a limited way. But Orthodoxy allowed for a personal interpretation, an accommodation in convictions, so long as the basic tenets of the faith allied. God revealed himself through His Word and through personal illumination. If Karen wanted her help, that was a kind of compliment.

"Are you having some kind of worry?" Meg said, low, since Karen walked several steps without speaking. Finances? Had John been laid off from his software company?

"I'm disturbed. Concerned," Karen said with a different emphasis. "You have renters in your house, don't you?"

"Yes. Busy young ladies with school and jobs," Meg said. She experienced a pang of regret that it wouldn't be possible for her to offer the family a place to stay if they couldn't meet their payments on their suburban tract house. Kids in the house would be chaotic but so much fun. She'd always wanted children.

"Then what I heard isn't right, I'm sure." Karen gave her a glowing smile.

No, she'd missed the mark. Karen meant something utterly different. Meg had a hard feeling in her stomach, like she needed food, or an antacid. She tried to keep her expression untroubled, but wondered how well she was doing. She'd never been able to keep what she felt off her face, but her conscience was clear, wasn't it?

"There are rumors in our church community that you have a *man* renting one of your rooms," Karen said. "I said it was really unlikely, but some of the mothers felt certain that they'd seen a man coming and going from your place in a regular fashion that could only be explained by his co-habiting with you. A tall man, drives a red truck. He must be working for you on the house? A contractor?"

"Wait a minute." Meg felt a flush heat her cheeks. She realized she could pretend that Dwayne was temporary labor, but she would not. Suddenly she felt old, tired, flabby.

"Co-habiting isn't the same as renting a room."

"But as a good Christian single woman, you could never justify having a single man under your roof... could you?"

"I certainly could. I do. I've invited a displaced man, Dwayne Wallace, into my garage for shelter. He had pneumonia and needed to sleep off the streets, in some place more sheltered than his old truck. That's all there is to it, Karen. I do have two other renters as well."

"But you know better than to house a man who's not related to you," Karen said.

"Better than to offer charity to a man down on his luck and sick unto death?"

"There must be other options, Mrs. Burdigal." Oh, so now it was Mrs. Burdigal, no longer Meg. "What you're doing is wrong. It presents a bad example, aside from the risk to your immortal soul. A false appearance. Anyone working for St. Athos Church needs to be aware of how they behave in public matters. You represent us."

Yes, Karen was on the Oversight Committee, her husband on the Homeless Outreach Panel. Meg felt her throat close so she had to swallow. She tried a slight smile, consciously relaxed her shoulders.

"You must see other people are deeply concerned. Mrs.

Burdigal. I can believe that in the pure goodness of your heart, you simply invited this man into your place for shelter. Even that nothing untoward has occurred so far. But you can't continue in this behavior and believe that we as a community will countenance it or that we can persist in believing the unlikely notion that nothing more is going on."

"Because I'm so needy and uncontrolled that I wouldn't be able to keep my hands off a homeless man?" The smile felt like overstrained elastic. She hated talking about Dwayne this way. He was clean when he had access to a shower, attractive and helpful. She thought of the shelves he planned to build in her garage, and how he'd fixed her kitchen sink.

"Please don't be crude, Mrs. Burdigal. The beauty of your soul is what matters. We want to support you. We are fellow Christians, your true family. Please don't push us away in our Christian concern. We only want to help."

"Judge not lest ye be judged," Meg said with as much dignity as she could.

"Beware of the sin that wears a handsome face," Karen said. "I can try to defend your reputation from your past mistake, but you must move this man to a more suitable accommodation immediately."

"My reputation from the past?"

"Your divorce," Karen hushed her voice; was that pity Meg heard? "I understand the division was powered by religious issues, which adds to your credit, but our church's view of divorce is …" she shrugged, her face grave, one hand touching her pregnant belly as though to protect it.

"My husband left for a secretary, Karen. Does that qualify as a religious difference?"

"I didn't mean to make you angry, but I forgive you. Your anger's understandable. We'll talk again, shall we? After you've had time for reflection."

As if she knew anything about it. Meg looked after Karen with the bitter knowledge that she was blushing, hot-faced standing here on this cold day. How could Karen imagine she could place Dwayne in a room the state provided, at a moment's notice? It had taken weeks to find shelter for her little family of Amalie and the two toddlers, renewable on a weekly basis. Even if she wanted to kick him back out, where could he go? Whose house was it, anyway?

She lifted her gaze to the tall eucalyptus, brushed in tawny gold, pink and olive, against the fog bank over the shore. Don't let Karen make you feel so trapped. The world God made is beautiful. Look at the branches move in the light stir of breeze; look at the colors, more vivid on this overcast day than in the blaze of afternoon. Colors fired by the glow of mist. The ocean beyond, green glass with surfer's wet heads bobbing. It's God's land. He knows what is right. He shall guide.

◆ 16 ◆

Jenny Pool could barely see the tops of palm trees and eucalyptus in the thickness of moisture. Past two A.M. in Freedom Park, the night stung with cold. No moon, but a clogging dampness from a low fog sucked itself in under trees, between bushes. Sea fog seemed always to make its own breeze, the drifts unwinding, moving over the grass, settling in layers. A plastic shopping bag moved whitish in the dim light, making rattling noises before it fetched up against a eucalyptus stump.

Charlie's dog, Boister, whined, maybe in his sleep, because he didn't get up. Charlie stretched over a sleep-slow arm to quiet him. The dog snuggled closer, sharing comfort; both sleepers stilled. Who, sleeping out tonight, wanted to move if they didn't have to? The fog sneaked in its damp touch between layers of clothes, even under blankets. The salt of sweat on unwashed fabric made the night cling colder.

Jenny Pool huddled herself in a hollow up against the eucalyptus stump. Some folk said low spots got chilly fast, but it meant she could get her covers completely over her, plus her knapsack. Then none of the bullies would be likely try to budge her from her spot. Charlie and Boister had never given her trouble. Maybe they'd even help if she needed it, but no one can ever count on much. Jenny lost her partner, Jim, last month to a massive stroke. Built like a brick shit house, with a temper that made him unemployable long years ago. Not much love lost between them, but he'd made warmth on bad nights, been her protection even if some nights she sniffled about the price.

Jenny flattened herself under the lee of the stump, settled in with all the edges as tucked in as she could manage. In a moment she woke herself, snoring a gin snore. Made her smile. She closed her eyes again, slipping into sleep.

◆ **17** ◆

Next morning in Freedom Park, Charlie was first up, sometime around six. A jogger with thudding feet, humming off key, woke him, then he couldn't get back to sleep even with Boister's fleabag warmth close by. Besides, he had to pee. That was the bad part about beer before bed. He scratched, made sure no one else was up to steal his stuff, went over by the eucalyptus stump.

God, that was better. But Jenny had been near here, hadn't she? OK, way over there, he saw her blankets, tossed aside, her knapsack lying near, but no Jenny. He wanted to take a fast peek inside her stuff—never know what someone might have to spare, but he was a good guy, wasn't he?

A good guy but damned hungry. Damned cold. Boister was hungry, too. He patted the brown head, smoothed the short flop ears, the dog grinned up at him. That duck they'd shared hadn't been half big enough. He might try for another in the park later today. Noisy, that was the problem. But God, there were a lot of ducks in Freedom Dogshit Park.

He could borrow a blanket, maybe, till Jenny got back. Wouldn't do any harm. He'd give it back. He looked around. No one else up and watching. He'd take care of Jenny's stuff for her, that was what. God, she'd been lying in a batch of duck shit. He picked up the knapsack with another fast look around and put it with his stuff, the blankets too, after shaking off the duck leavings. Boister wrinkled his nose, snuffling the knapsack, whining. Smelled nasty, it did. She'd be glad he was taking care of her belongings. Maybe she had the runs or something, hiding in the bushes now. He'd wait a while. Too goddamned early for breakfast at the Havens anyhow.

◆ **18** ◆

"Mrs. Meg? Can I talk to you?"

Charlie again. What problem had he brought her this time? She saw his nose was running—it was probably too cold for him to feel it. He hunched over next to the table, his goods and his dog by his feet.

"Get yourself something to eat," she said, "then we can talk." Funny what a good mood she was in. Bring on the problems. Meg felt like she could solve anything today, even that nagging issue of Karen's suspicions about Dwayne. "I need a cup myself. Oh, and Charlie? There's some dog kibble a guy donated back in the trailer. Let me get it for Boister."

"Thanks, Mrs. Meg," Charlie said. "You're the greatest."

A little later Meg sat where she could keep a sharp eye on the table. Only peanut butter sandwiches today, some with jelly, but if she didn't watch, stacks had a way of vanishing under a guy's clothes. Not fair to the others when that happened. Boister ate eagerly, crunching the kibble with strong white teeth—much better teeth than his poor master, who ate his sandwich as though it had bones in it. She could see he only half chewed before he swallowed, gulping. Maybe she could try to match him up for one of the free dental clinics. Charlie could be touchy. Hey, couldn't they all?

"So what's the problem?" she said, warming her fingers on the ceramic mug of weak coffee.

"I have some stuff I hadn't ought to have," he said, and winced over his coffee. She wanted to say something about how hot things could hurt a sore tooth but hesitated. What sort of thing might he have? Contraband? Drugs?

"Mmm?" she said, inviting more, but careful not to demand.

"Have you seen Jenny Pool anywhere around?"

"I can't recall...maybe not for a couple of days?"

"Something's happened to her." Charlie opened his huge duffel and pried out the familiar faded knapsack. "I found this two days ago right by the place where she went to sleep the night before. Her blankets got left too. Waited around a while but she never came back, so I thought I'd take care of her stuff for her. But I ain't seen anything of her, and no one I ask seems to know."

Meg put down her coffee on the table, her stomach turning over with dread. She accepted the knapsack, but she couldn't help wanting to hold it away from her. She compromised by setting it on the table.

"I'll need to tell the police," she said. "I worry when someone disappears like this without her belongings. I appreciate your telling me. You know, though, two years ago we had a disappearance, and you remember what happened that time?"

"Oh, you mean Sandra?" His face lit at the memory.

Of course, Meg should have assumed any bit of hope, any good story, got passed from hand to hand and heart to heart in this community. They all wanted a happy ending.

"Yes." It did no harm to repeat a fine thing. "Her family found her. They wanted her back. She'd run away thinking they hated her for something she'd done, but they were all so happy to be back together. She left everything, even half a bag of potato chips."

They smiled at each other. Then the frown returned to Charlie's face.

"Can I keep her blankets… for now? Would it do any harm? And… and I drank her gin."

Probably used any money you found. There but for the grace of God. Judge not lest ye be judged. Meg nodded. Whatever had happened to Jenny's stuff was between Charlie, Jenny and God. That he'd made this much of a confession was good enough for now.

◆◆◆

"God damn it," Officer Rudy said, rapping his pencil on his notepad. "Mrs. Meg, don't you even know when to get in out of the rain? What're the odds the guy whacked her, took her stuff and…"

"No." Meg passed him a mug of coffee. Coffee helped so many things.

"Who was it?"

"Charlie. You know him."

"Yeah, yeah I do," Officer Rudy said. He accepted the mug and sipped carefully at the steaming edge. His broad black face had the old scars of acne and his eyes the red rims of a man who doesn't sleep well. She looked at his thick fingers gripping the mug handle and shook her head.

"Now what are you disapproving of me for?" he said.

"Jumping to judgment. As soon as I said Charlie—"

"Well, well. It's a sure thing if he went and killed someone, Charlie would be in screaming bad shape. I'd be carting him to the County mental, that's what. Can't say the same of them all." He nodded at the group of men and women sitting about, each at a certain distance from the others under the cheerful red flowers of the bottle-brush trees. Mrs. Fuller hunched over her stack of bags, chewing on something, her head tilted. Colin waved a hand when he spoke to Ilene, Winsome, and Ginny. Dwayne leaned against the trunk of the biggest tree, looking down at the others. He was going to make her shelves for the garage. He seemed handy with tools, ready for work, and always with a positive word to share. She wondered what his full story was. Dwayne hinted sometimes at parts of his past, told a tale now and again, but she didn't have a full picture yet.

A lot of folk on the road these days, so many displaced by circumstances beyond their control. Sure, there were plenty in the mental health category, and a lot of drug addictions and booze stories, but then there were the crushing divorces, the missed connections, the man whose business got embezzled into the ground by his best friend, the other whose wife ran off with a lover and the family bank account. So many with health costs they couldn't meet, often a spouse dead of cancer but all the chemo bills to meet. Look at her own experience, nursing Dad, fielding his bills until he died. Her husband had been tired of "life in a fucking nursing home" as he put it, and left with his secretary, leaving the debt Medicare didn't cover. No one told you that Medicare didn't pay for all the chemotherapy, until way late in the process. But how could you refuse chemo for your dad?

Dwayne had already fixed the leaky faucet on the garden hose and rehung the door to her kitchen cabinet. He stared at someone, so Meg shifted in her seat until she could see whom he watched. A tall cadaverous man stood silent to one side, his clothes gapping around him. Even from here they looked stiff with ground-in dirt, the kind that takes months or years to acquire. His mouth a little open, his arms wrapped around his middle.

"Who's that?" she said, distracted. "I don't know him. He looks like he needs more than a sandwich."

"You know the law, ma'am," Officer Rudy said.

"Yes," she said, watching the stranger; he now seemed to try to laugh with the others, two beats too slow. Dwayne said something that made the others laugh harder and the new man tried again, but he drooped almost immediately afterwards, looking down at his feet as though he knew it was a lost cause.

"I need to welcome him," Meg said.

"I'll talk to Charlie, but I'm impounding this knapsack of Jenny's and contents. I'll give you a receipt. Did she leave anything else?"

"Some blankets." Meg dusted off her hands, "but I told Charlie he could keep them."

"Mrs. Meg, you drive me crazy. There could be evidence…. We gotta get those back."

"I'm sorry," she said. "I didn't think about that. I should have, I know. Charlie was headed out on Tokeham Road looking for bottles, he said."

"I'll go after. Catch you up later. Call my cell if you see him in the next hour in case he hides like the last time I went looking."

"Last time you were taking bad news to him, and he knew it. We've had no trouble with Boister these last few weeks. Don't worry Charlie, please? He's… tender."

"Do my best," Officer Rudy said.

❖ 19 ❖

Dad was home. Nicole had thought it would make all the difference. For a few hours it did, until he told her how soon the next panel meeting would be.

"Why can't they ever meet in California?" she said. "Why can't they confer by phone? How can all these important people give up their time to get on a jet and waste hours getting to DC? Think of the carbon footprint."

"Some of them live on the East Coast. Some of them live in DC. Some like the thrill of waiting in line, squeezing into a narrow seat to fly in a mailing tube across the country." Mom set down the bowl of hot rolls before she went back to the kitchen.

"Because." Dad raised his bristly eyebrows, looking even more like Harpo Marx, but with a sound track. Or Vonnegut with blond fuzzy hair minus moustache. "Because Washington DC is special, with special traffic, special pollution, special noise—"

"Sounds like Isla Vista." Mom brought in a pot of stew. Smelled wonderful. Mom's food always did, even when she had the strangest ingredients. Nicole still thought of tofu as a glamorized eraser even though she'd been raised on the stuff. But this was real meat tonight, with fat mushrooms glazed in a sauce smelling of balsamic vinegar and caramelized onions. Nicole reached for an oatmeal roll fresh from the oven, Mom style. Dad often said that Mom brought her chemistry to her kitchen.

"I read the Lovecraft I found at The Book Nook," Nicole said.

"Stay up all night?" Mom buttered her own roll with the same precision she brought to everything. Not a drop of melting butter escaped.

"Was asleep before two, but I sure had weird dreams," Nicole said. "What was your favorite Lovecraft story, Mom?"

"Don't remember…remind me."

"'Rats in the Walls,' 'Dunwich Horror,' 'Color out of—'"

"Color Out of Space." Both Mom and Dad spoke in unison. "Absolutely the best."

"Hah," Nicole said. "Now I know why you got married."

"That was a story without a conscience," Mom said. "No one safe. No act of kindness, humanity or faith could save anyone from that alien. No happy ending. Best concept ever."

"Do you think aliens would be like that?" Nicole said. She stuffed another large forkful of tender beef and gravy into her mouth.

"Could be. Depends if they come to satisfy curiosity and hope, or a simply a need for resources. Instinctive behavior or intellectual, plus the question of whether they have any care for fellow sentients if they themselves are sentient."

"Funny you ask that," Dad said. "There were two proposals about defending Earth from alien invasion. Funny stuff, not based in good science, but the proposal authors would love this conversation."

"This isn't a *non sequitur*, but I got my first results from your PCR machine, Dad."

"I hope Sam didn't—"

"I did it myself. Well, ninety-eight percent of it. Sam says they're for shit," Nicole said. "The results that is. Make no sense. Repetitive errors, would be terminal in a real animal."

"Must have been contaminated. It's easy to have that happen when you're not used to the protocols."

"I know them by heart. Want to hear?"

"No." Mom smiled when she said it. Nicole took a bite of beef melting in sauce, a dribble sneaking down her chin. Napkin to the rescue.

"So you think you ran a clean lab?" Dad said.

"Clean as clean can be," Nicole said.

"Let me have a look after dinner. Maybe I can tell you what might have happened."

"Thanks," Nicole managed and settled into serious eating. If food was chemistry, she should learn to do better than a "B". But chemistry was so boring the way it was taught in high school.

"What kinds of proposals are you deciding to fund—or not to fund—in the meetings?" Mom asked.

"Everything from the Spaghetti Monster to some studies right here in California. Ocean rifts. Black smokers. You may recall the finding of a bacterium in saline conditions at Mono Lake where they claimed arsenic substituted for phosphorous in the DNA. They're still fighting over that one. We saw a proposal to revisit that study."

"What else?"

"All kinds of speculations on alien life and the possibilities, what nucleotides might substitute for adenine, cytosine, guanine and thymine."

"What else is out there, and possible?" Nicole said. She buttered her roll, her heart pounding. She knew she'd done a clean procedure and Sam had watched. What if there were strange reasons for her lab procedures not working?

"Do we know?" Dad shrugged. "Possible to see a three-bit code instead of our four, a nucleotide like tetrahymena might be a possible substitute. But you'd want stability in the system, nucleotides that don't alter under thermic stress changes. So while you're asking questions instead of letting me pig out, here's one for you, Nic. Why don't any of the organisms on earth have a different number of something different from our standard nucleotides? Plenty of possible nucleotides out there…"

"Horizontal transfer," Nicole said. "But Dad… in alien life, not earth life, couldn't we have something like XNA instead of DNA?"

"I suppose. You want to write the next proposal my panel has to review?"

"PNA, LNA?"

"TNA or GNA," Mom said. "Sounds good, kid."

After dinner, Nicole surrendered her print-outs to Dad. He was quiet for a while. She could tell from the stillness in his pointed face that he was disappointed.

"Contaminants. I'm sorry. That's the only possible parsimonious explanation."

"But look, Dad. Look at that."

Now he had a much more promising frown.

"You've been doing what with my machine?"

"Everything under Sam's watchful eye. You know he loves your PCR better than his girlfriend."

"He has a girlfriend?"

"I dunno. I said that, but maybe the PCR is his girl these days. I caught him petting it."

"So Nic, what are you proposing?"

"I got this sample from Mrs. Meg's house. Did Mom tell you about her coming over and ranting like a PETA advocate? Said she had something in her house that had to be a lab mutation—something nasty the University labs had created using vivisection, and from what she said, it looked like part mammal, part jellyfish, with blue eyes. She had us go back to her house to see."

"And you went over and found the source in a bottle of gin."

"No." Mom brought in a plate of sliced pears. "I think she's too inhibited to indulge in more than the occasional glass of wine. She was shaken, ran over here in her stocking feet, but when we went home with her we found nothing but a wet spot on the carpet."

"Like someone had dumped the jello for a church social there, but no fruity smell. Smelled rotten in fact," Nicole said.

"She has dogs; who knows what—"

"She said the thing had tabby fur, and I found a bit near the jello wet spot. With skin." Nicole watched Dad.

That detail caught Dad's attention.

"With skin?"

Nicole nodded. "So that's what I processed for the PCR. And you have the results."

Dad said nothing. He took a piece of pear and bit it as though the act was something to do, rather than prompted by appetite. Nicole looked at Mom and saw her grin, with a fierce satisfaction that had nothing to do with pears.

"OK, I need to know if you really understand your biology of inheritance, Nic. Tell me how it works, please," Dad said.

"DNA is a neutral or passive report of what has managed to survive on earth. It's like the memory of life, with some gaps like memory loss."

"Whom are you plagiarizing, Nic?"

"A forum on the internet."

"Get me the web address, please. I'm going to use that site in class," Mom said.

"OK, Nicole," Dad nodded to himself. "We'll run your samples again, Alien Scientist."

"I don't have much left," Nicole said, worried now. "In fact, just a tiny scrap's all."

"Where'd you keep it?"

"In our fridge in a glass vial; sorry Mom," she said. "I didn't want anyone in the lab to toss it out."

"Who, me, object to mysterious bits of dead animals in my kitchen?"

"Wait 'til I clean up all the crap that's waiting for me at the office, and we'll get on it. Look Nic, I really don't think Mrs. Meg had an alien in her living room, but it'll be fun to check your protocols. OK?"

As long as he really got around to it. Nicole took a nice juicy slab of pear and munched. The phone rang, and annoyance touched Mom's face.

"I'll get it," Nicole said. It was the least she could do.

"Hello? This is Mr. Marks, the Biology teacher at San Marcos High School. Is this Nicole?"

"Yes, it is," she said, her throat tightening as if she'd done something wrong.

"I know it's unusual to call you out of school, but I wanted to break this to you so you'd have time to accommodate."

A scholarship? It was too soon. She hadn't applied to anything yet.

"Are you still there, Nicole?"

"Yes."

"There's a new student in our biology class, a late transfer. He's way behind on the science project, and so I'm assigning him to work with you."

"No."

"His name is Jack Kushner. He was an 'A' student at his previous high school. You will work as his partner. This is not optional. You need to adjust your attitude," he said. Now something in his voice told her he'd come to that point which weak men reach where he would treat the least negative sound as a full rebellion. She had a vision of Mr. Marks wheeling out a cannon and aiming it at their front door, frothing at the mouth with all the rage of a defied High School Biology teacher. She decided to say nothing. She set the receiver down gently, because if she acted right now upon her feelings, she'd break it.

This Jack Kushner was going to regret all his life that his family had decided to move to Isla Vista, California. Might not be entirely his fault that he was parachuting in on top of her project, but he was going to wish he'd never heard of her.

◆ 20 ◆

Brian found himself smiling at the small brown dog scampering across the garage floor to greet him, claws skittering. So awkward and fuzzy, more like a toy than a canine. When it bounced to the door Brian cast a quick glance around. No sign of a mistake, no turds, no yellow puddles.

"Good dog." He opened the door to his small back yard. The dog flung itself out, raced to the back and took a long pee. What would he call it? Longpee didn't cut it as a name.

Brian stood in the doorway, breathing the exhaust mixed with sea breeze that filled Isla Vista. The sun already dipped low, the clouds on the horizon shaded to pink. He'd take the pup out, take a walk along the beach. The vet had said the dog was healthy except for worms, and not a puppy at all, despite its small size. She said probably some college student had left it behind. Brian had to fight to keep his anger down. College students took on a pet like a new pillow for the sofa, then shed a living animal behind like trash, surrounding the animal's probable fate with some rosy tinted fantasy about it living a good free life by the beach. All you had to do was look at the homeless to see such pretty thinking was a lie.

Halloween was around the corner. Should be a doozie this year with drunk kids and not-quite adults strewn about like the corpses on a battlefield. Brian hadn't planned much except to keep himself and the dog in. Might take a stroll to see what the costumes on the main street looked like. How many girls dressed in nothing but body paint with sequins. Halloween was one of those traditions dating from the sixties when this university boasted a reputation for parties and surfing, not study and laboratories.

"No sleeping this weekend," he warned the dog. "Our street will vibrate under your paws—the walls will shake while the whole world rushes into Isla Vista to party, then leaves us with all the crap to clean up."

◆ 21 ◆

Meg paused on her way back to the sink. She looked over at Dwayne. He stood to put back his chair, ready to return to his garage.

"Have you seen Mrs. Fuller recently?" Meg said. "I had an appointment to take her back to County Health to check her infected foot, but I can't find her. No one seems sure where she might be. First Jenny vanishes, now Sadie."

"Search me," Dwayne said. "You know, I've been here most of the time, watching the lungs. Sadie wasn't our easiest lady to get along with. One hell of a temper on her, you know? But I'm a man of peace now," Dwayne said. "My violent days are over. I was a bad actor once upon a time, but now I've seen the light, you might say. I'm a reformed man. You know, I even walked away from a job a couple months back because this other guy who wanted it real bad began to make threats. I decided I wasn't the kind of guy who would come to cuffs over a stupid job. Speaking of that, I better get myself to work if I'm going to finish those shelves in your garage before November."

"Take another cookie with you," Meg said.

"Don't mind if I do." Dwayne reached out both hands, though, and caught her empty one as well as the one with the cookie, holding both in his large strong fingers before he let go, slipping the cookie into his palm. He gave her a grin, then sauntered back down the hall to the garage.

Manners, she said to herself. He had such good manners. Always gave her little attentions, like drawing out her chair before dinner, attentions she'd thought forgotten by almost everyone but her. He was so much more refined than the gossipy members of St. Athos Church could imagine.

Yes, manners. She had to go make a call on her neighbors, the Carlquists. Poor Nicole must have been shocked. What had she been thinking, rushing in like that and firing off accusations of evil doings at the university laboratories? That's what came of talking for two hours earlier with Charlie, who was convinced the university stalked his dog Boister, with an intention of teaching him to fetch bombs. God knew that she'd meant no harm, but it surely hadn't come out of her mouth that way. Oh dear, look at the clock. She'd be late to work at this rate.

◆ ◆ ◆

After returning home from work, Meg baked and stacked a generous plate of fat chocolate chip cookies, still a bit on the gooey side. Everyone liked them that way. She took a deep breath. Right thing to do. Yes, she had to say she was sorry and thank Mrs. Carlquist and Nicole for coming over to help her the other day. They must think she was crazy. She should ask them if they'd seen her cat, Schrand, around. She'd already called the local animal rescues and the County Animal Shelter three times each. Spent an hour wakeful last night, imagining what might have happened to him.

Out the door. She kept herself on track, not allowing doubts to turn her back. Yes, some said least said, soonest mended, but her faith believed in confession and repentance. That reminded her that she'd meant to call Father Stephens and talk about the gossip at the church. He hadn't spoken with her, so she knew he wasn't troubled. Not yet, at least. But she'd be wise to take his measure on what she was doing and be assured her motives were pure.

She recalled Dwayne's warm hands holding hers for that moment this morning, the slight movement of his thumb like a caress, and she wondered at herself. Did Dwayne mean anything by those little gestures? Or was it all simple gratitude for her timely help? She stopped in her tracks; a pedestrian behind her brushed her before skipping to the side and passing.

What was she thinking? That she wanted more than gratitude?

"Mrs. Burdigal," said a light female voice, familiar, and Meg jerked back to present reality and the sidewalk where she stood, the draggled jacaranda tree bare over her head and the pedestrian who'd gone by now hurried on without a backwards look. She looked at the girl standing under the jacaranda.

"Nicole?" she said.

"Are you OK?"

"Sure, sure I am. I was walking over to see you and your mother," Meg said.

"What's wrong?" Nicole sounded wary and no wonder.

"I owe an apology to you both, and thanks, and some cookies," Meg said.

"Why ever?" Nicole shook her head, the untidy black hair shaking out around her narrow face. She smiled, probably relieved that Meg wasn't going into some weird rant. "Come on in." Nicole ran along the last few steps on the grass before hopping to the sidewalk where her hedge began.

Meg heard a mew, a rusty pitiful sound coming from under the hedge between properties. With abrupt hope she looked around, following the sound.

"Did you hear that?" she said.

"What?"

"A cat. I heard a cat."

Nicole came to her, accepted the plate of covered cookies. Meg paused, bent over to peer under the Eugenia bushes that hedged the Carlquists' front yard. She hadn't realized how much she'd worried about Schrand until this moment. He'd disappeared for a few days before now and again, but never this long. She imagined the mew familiar, known, and dear, and breathed a prayer under her breath so she wouldn't embarrass Nicole by calling on God aloud.

Eyes—she caught the glint of them when the animal under the thicket turned its head.

"Schrand? Is that you, my poor fellow?"

She couldn't see much. Then Nicole set her knapsack and the plate down and came near, but a step behind Meg. She moved slowly, kneeling on the cold stones before making a deep funny sound that came somewhere between a purr and a chirrup.

"Puss?" Nicole said. She made the sound again and the animal came a few steps out. It couldn't be Schrand, Meg thought. The right sort of color, but dirty as only a sick cat will let itself be. Then he tilted his head and looked up at her and she gasped.

"It is you," she said. He flinched and fled back into the bushes.

"I'll get some tuna," said Nicole. "I didn't know you had a tail-less cat, Mrs. Burdigal."

It took another series of attempts before Meg finally cradled her cat. Postman Brian came by the mailbox and stopped on seeing them.

"Good God," Brian said. "What's happened to your cat, Mrs. Meg? Who hurt him? Did the dogs?"

"Never," Meg said, feeling the tears start down her face. "I'd never let them...."

She turned around and started for home, Brian's face swimming in the tears that fell from her eyes. How could he imagine she'd let her dogs hurt her cat? Schrand didn't like being held, usually, but now he pressed his body against hers, his purr a loud anxious song of pain and pleading. The stump of his tail had been peeled, and it hurt Meg to look down at it. She'd have to get the vet to fix the stub, amputate that pitiful naked bit.

"I'll walk with you," Nicole's breathless voice came from behind her, "in case Schrand decides to make a break for it. I had to put my stuff and the cookies inside first. I'm sorry, Meg, Brian didn't know what had happened. He says he'll see you tomorrow, and he's really sorry about Schrand. Are you dating Brian?"

"No," Meg said. "No he means the mail, Nicole, don't be silly."

"Too bad." Nicole sounded unrepentant about her hint that Meg and Brian might be involved. She seemed to be deliberately ignoring Meg's tears. Maybe she thought what she said was funny and a good diversion. It wasn't.

❖ 22 ❖

Shorty Winsome glanced around the beach and dunes before he unpacked. No one out here. The last of long, late light glimmered in the tops of waist-high scrub, glittering on the white tops out to sea. The surf sounded near; high tide. The shadows already held a cold that bit deep.

After checking for watchers one more time, he knelt. He wriggled along a narrow passage into the crooked bushes that anchored the land-side dunes, pulled his bundles after him through the shallow scramble until he reached the inside by the clustered roots where he'd scraped and hollowed a nice place to sleep. Big enough to scrabble around in. Not perfect, but down out of the wind. Winsome painstakingly tugged the plastic ground sheet out then laid his oldest blanket over it.

If he ate a candy bar after he settled, that would make for some good warmth in a bit. Who'd taught him that trick? Couldn't remember. But tonight he had a Snickers from the dumpster back of Ralph's. He'd had words with the black dude, the newcomer from San Diego. Told him this was Winsome's place to forage even if it was a lie. No one owned much; it was all first come unless you were a big guy like that Dwayne.

God, Dwayne was sitting pretty now, living with Mrs. Meg. Some folk said they were doing the nasty, but he didn't believe it. Mrs. Meg did everything by the Book. Besides, it was, as she'd have said, a blessing. With Dwayne off the street, Winsome had a better chance of keeping this hide to himself.

He put some valuables deep in his roll, the expired driver's license, a ring that might be silver, his envelope of photos, and a couple of letters. He checked his cash, tucking it in the shirt breast pocket under his jacket even though this was such a good spot he reckoned he was about as safe as could be from the other guys on the street and the Isla Vista Foot Patrol. Worse than the regular cops, that IVFP. Jumped-up college students with badges and walkie-talkies, tattling back and forth. Winsome could see what came along the path from this hidey hole, and so long as he didn't snore at the wrong time, he'd be OK.

He arranged himself carefully and pulled out the candy, leaning on his elbows in the cocoon of wraps he'd tucked up. Already his legs felt the warmth reflecting in, though it'd take a while for his feet to get comfortable. Winsome peeled back the wrapper on the bar then slowly sniffed the chocolate smell with the hint of nuts. He'd had his sandwich earlier, but the odor of sweet and chocolate made his mouth water. Winsome took a nibble off that perfect smooth brown corner, let the chocolate melt on the tip of his tongue. Nothing like sugar to keep your blood moving.

Dark night, no moon coming, the bushes rattling overhead with the wind from the sea. That was the bad part about this spot. The noise from the sea. It could mask other important noises, like people talking. Made him smile to think of the tall dormitories a couple hundred feet away from where he lay, snug as a bug in a rug. All those students without a clue that he was here right near them in his own dormitory room, the same ocean sounding on the sand, the same wind buffeting.

Something moved outside while he chewed. White, rushing suddenly across the dune beyond the entrance to his nest. Winsome tried to get it into focus, already guessing. One of those fucking plastic shopping bags. He'd heard they were going to outlaw those things. He watched it in the twilight cross his entrance then pass again.

Something wrong about that? Well, the wind went crossways sometimes. Eddies. He saw it again, closer. Entertaining; he had his own personal TV tonight. Some nights he saw rats, but tonight it was a shopping bag. Getting nice and warm now, the fingers licked clean of chocolate and tucked into his armpits.

Winsome's view cut off. Goddamn plastic bag. He didn't want to move his fingers from their cozy place, but he didn't like the way the bag made him feel, as if the door had closed. He waited for the wind to budge it, but the wind didn't seem to be catching the plastic. With a groan, Winsome drew his hand out and reached down his little tunnel, hitching forward a couple of inches, trying to keep all the blankets in place. A little further. He stretched his hand at full extension, finally snagging the bag.

Ow. So cold. The freezing contact hurt, the pain radiating up along his arm from where his fingers had hooked into the gelid form. He heard his own choking sound, oddly muffled, agony intense, like a burn, like acid on his skin. The white floppy shape seemed to be pulling itself up his arm, expanding, enveloping, burning wet and clinging. He thought he was shaking his arm, whipping it back and forth, but he saw his arm didn't move.

Winsome couldn't move. In his mind, he'd leapt to his feet

having given every alarm to his body, but he still lay prone with the white billow growing, sliding up his arm. Expanding. The nearest edge was agony, hand and arm numbed as it progressed. He could see through the translucent bag surface how his clothes dissolved, the brown plaid flannel fraying, the pink skin and black hair on his arm turning red, then melting paler as if the blood simply vanished, streaks of other colors, the veins there, then gone, the white of bone, and then nothing but a swirl of fluids. Winsome couldn't scream; there was no drawing of breath, even as his lungs ached for air. The chill wet lunged into his face. He tried to scream. Oh, he was getting away, wasn't he? So slow and dreamy. The flare of pain faded. He believed his feet hit solid ground. Wasn't he screaming? He heard nothing more at all.

◆ 23 ◆

"Have you seen Winsome around, Dwayne?" Meg put another ladle of soup into his bowl. He ate whatever she served with appreciation. She liked to see that—it made her feel profoundly content. He never complained that she was skimping on the meat. He probably had no idea how cheap she could keep what came to table. The surgery on poor Schrand's tail had cost an unexpected couple of hundred dollars. Schrand still acted as though he thought he was a leper, hiding under the furniture.

"Nope. Winsome's not the sort of guy I'd expect you to miss, know what I mean?"

She wasn't sure why she cringed at that. Dwayne was only being funny, and the good Lord knew a lot of the homeless folk and their stories had elements of humor as much as tragedy. He was one of them, after all; maybe that gave him license to make fun. She shouldn't be so uptight. Should she say something or keep her mouth shut?

"I look at his back, and I wonder if some of his nastier cracks come from it hurting him," she compromised.

"Meg, you need to lighten up," Dwayne said. He took another slice of bread and buttered it, lavishly. It was good to see him enjoy what he ate. Maybe she could find some cheaper butter if she went to one of the larger stores, but then there was the question of gasoline to get there. She always watched those things. Everything added up. Like sin.

"Lighten up and not worry so much. God doesn't care if we make a few jokes."

"I worry about being cruel. Even in thought. Maybe that's a bit over the top."

"It sure is," Dwayne said. "You live about as holy a life as I can bear."

He grinned at her as if to make what he said a joke.

"I've always wanted to do what's right," she said.

"I bet." He put the last crust into his mouth. "It shows. You ever have much fun? I imagine you as the quiet girl in class, always waiting to be called on."

"Pretty much true," she said, but something about that stung.

"You're a good woman, Meg," he said with that softer look she liked on his face. He considered her until she had to look away.

"Your ex-husband was a fool," he said.

"Well, I always thought that."

He laughed. "Good. Good to know that you'll stick up for yourself. You should like yourself when so many other people do. I do," he said. "In fact, every time I see you—"

"What?" She was full of tremulous curiosity and a kind of hope. Dwayne shook his head.

"Oh crap, I remembered I need to get some more supplies. I need to finish measuring. Don't come in before I'm done," he said. "I'm not good with too much supervision."

She started the dishes, found herself smiling a lot, turning the fork and spoon Dwayne had used over in her hands before putting them into the soapy water. Her plump hands looked so unfinished somehow, like a girl's, no lovely taper. When the phone rang, she started.

"Mrs. Burdigal? Yes, I'm the pharmacist at the CVS Drugstore at Gutierrez. Carmen Cortez, here. Yesterday, Ilene Gordon left me a note that as Homeless Outreach Coordinator you requested an upgrade in the medication quantity prescribed to her. I told her she needs to contact the physician for an authorization for any change in her medications. It is outside of your authority. In fact, I suspect she didn't consult you, but since I cannot reach her at the number she gave, I thought I'd try you since you seem to know her."

"I do. She hasn't a local primary physician. She uses the County—"

"Whatever. Doctors write all prescriptions, and it has to be on record."

"I know she really does need more medication than her present prescription. She doesn't have enough pills for a month. She runs out." Meg wasn't about to admit that she hadn't tried to authorize anything.

"The number I see here should be adequate. She must be selling them."

"No, she's not. She's in need of more pain relief than she's getting. She's sleeping in the bushes or on a park bench, Ms. Cortez. There's no mattress, and she has significant pain due to arthritis, a pair of collapsed discs and lumbar spines pinching her nerves."

"Sounds like she needs surgery, not more medication."

"Of course she does." Even as she spoke, Meg knew she should stop. This was headed nowhere good. "She can't afford it. She may look like she's ninety, but she's not under Medicare yet. She's forty-eight and never declared incapacity because she still has dreams of finding a job taking care—"

"Don't be naïve. These people sell their prescriptions for booze, Mrs. Burdigal. You surely must know that in your position. I see you're at Saint Athos's Church, so maybe they pay you to think the best of everyone, but if you gave the homeless all the drugs they want, they'd overdose. She can apply for disability."

"They buy the booze to kill the pain of medications that aren't enough to help a dog, Ms. Cortez, because you people won't trust them with enough to help."

She heard the phone slam down. Great, Meg; she set her receiver back in its cradle. How to win friends and influence care protocols. Between all the people at the church who seemed to be too busy to talk with her, and losing her temper with the pharmacist, she was definitely having a great week. To make it even better, Halloween loomed. Another year, she might have tried to leave town for the weekend, but she didn't have the budget for that, not with an extra mouth to feed and a vet bill. Not that she minded those, of course.

❖ 24 ❖

Nicole met Jack Kushner when she came into the Biology lab for Mr. Marks's class. Lean, depressed-looking, he had too-long brown hair and heavy eyebrows. Thrift shop leather jacket, blue jeans. Handsome, in a geeky sort of way. Sullen, or maybe defensive as a new guy at a new school had every right to be.

"I'm Nicole." She shucked her knapsack onto the floor by her stool.

"Are you really going to vivisect and toast me on the Bunsen Burner for lunch?"

"Depends how much of an asshole you are," she said. "Who's been telling tales?" If he knew what a Bunsen Burner did, they were way ahead of the curve already.

"Everyone. They said, 'Don't worry about the gym teacher, or the math and computer science teacher with a habit of torturing flies, and the French teacher's a sweetie, but your lab partner is *scary*.'"

"I am. Don't forget it. You mess up, and you and the Bunsen will discover an intimate relationship. Why did your family move here?"

He scowled at her with abrupt venom.

"Mind you own business, Princess Nerd."

She shrugged. What got his goat? She'd been thinking he might be tolerable until he got his underpants in a twist over her first real question.

Later in the day, Nicole found him turning up in all of her classes: AP English, AP French, AP History. Thank God he wasn't in her gym class. But after sixth period, she bumped into him hanging out in the hall where he was trying to have a conversation with two guys she knew were important in basketball.

"Nicole," he said. He waved goodbye to the boys.

She didn't speak but stopped in her tracks, looked hard at him.

"Yes, you're right," he said. "I'm an asshole. I apologize for snapping at you."

"I wasn't trying to pry," she said after a moment of wondering how best to say what she felt. "I'm no good at small talk, but even now I don't know what I said that pissed you off."

"Nothing," he said. "Not your fault. I think that your mother is supposed to know my mother."

"How?" Nic said.

"Work. She's in a lab at the university. See you tomorrow." He made the same gesture he'd just made to the guys and veered off across the corridor to the outside door.

"Huh," she said after him. "Guess your social skills aren't any better than mine."

Hadn't mom said something about an old friend moving into town? So this was the son. Oh God, then she didn't have full freedom to be as rude as she liked. Or did she?He stopped.

"Yeah," he said. "Takes one to know one. Where are you headed?"

"To the lab," she said. "I'm not inviting you."

He fell into step with her when she passed him as if he hadn't heard, but when she looked at him, scowling her best scowl, he was watching his feet. When she turned west down Camino Pescadero, he continued alongside. Ignoring him had to be the best policy, so Nicole stopped walking in the high school dawdling way she used when on the high school campus. She put some push into it, swinging along in the fashion that her friends said verged on jogging. Jack kept up.

Passing Mrs. Meg's house, she saw Postman Brian, gave him a wave and smile that faded when she saw a man watching from Mrs. Meg's doorway. Wasn't that man the big bully she'd met in the bookstore?

Maybe Postman Brian knew something she didn't. She caught up with him, Jack keeping pace.

"Hey," Nicole said to Brian. Not sure what to call him, though she knew his name. "Postman" didn't seem polite. "Who's that guy in Mrs. Meg's house?"

"Dwayne Wallace," Brian said, giving a slight smile to Jack. "And who's this?"

"Isn't Dwayne on the streets?"

"Used to be," Brian said in a way that made her feel she'd vexed him. "Got pneumonia, so Mrs. Meg moved him into her garage."

"I wouldn't have," Nicole said. "Pneumonia or not. He's no good. Mean."

Brian shrugged. "Mrs. Meg thinks he's great. That's all what matters. And where are your manners? Who's this rival for your affections?"

Nicole was horrified. How could he be dumb enough to say something like that?

"This is my best enemy," she said. "Jack Kushner. Moved in on top of my territory. Now I'm forced to work on my science project with him."

"See you later," Jack said and extended his own stride to something Nicole would have had trouble matching. He bore off down a side street as if he knew where he was going, though he probably didn't. Nicole knew it was a dead end.

"Damn," Nicole said.

"Did I do something?" Brian said.

"Of course." Honesty forced her to add, "but way less than I did."

She continued on her way to the university campus, gnawing on her conscience the whole way. But mom should know better than trying to arrange play dates with other kids when they were this old. Doomed to failure. Mom and her friend should bug out of Nicole and Jack's business.

◆ **25** ◆

Charlie said Freedom Park, or Dogshit Park if you prefer, had no mice left for Boister to snap after, and the few rats ran nervous in a way their easy Southern Californian lifestyle didn't explain. Used to be Boister could catch a couple when times were rough and Charlie hadn't much extra for him, but recently Charlie had to go short to keep his dog fed. He'd thought about ducks, but though they once crowded the pond in the middle of the park, only twenty or so remained, and the quack among ducks might now be about moving on to better quarters.

Charlie decided someone must have dumped toxic waste in the pond. The government always did things like that. The ducks flew at a side-ways look, like someone'd been scaring them. But the good news was he didn't sleep, these nights, at the park. Charlie had discovered a new place to nest down, across Isla Vista a block from the Garden and Pool Supply. Ilene hung out there, too, and Rapper as well.

When Rapper was on your side he was a great buddy, and not

even the big guys like Dwayne crossed him, because no one knew if Rapper had an off switch. Rapper'd been in a good place in his mind these last few weeks, and it was fun to hear him go on and on like a professional, near as good as the radio, except what he rapped about was the life they were all leading. He was damned funny. Charlie hoped the good mood would last.

Spooky the way Winsome disappeared. Winsome never talked about moving on, so what had happened to change his plans? This was a good time to have a tough friend; no one would mess with them while they were with Rapper.

◆ 26 ◆

Something was happening over there. Meg turned her head, fast, getting to her feet before she quite registered the two men facing each other. Timid Sam had gone off—his normally shrunk-in posture changed, expanded. He exuded dangerous readiness.The big fellow facing him hadn't caught on.

"Friends," Meg said, loud, so it would carry across the space she crossed. "Gentlemen, may I offer you a cup of coffee?"

The big fellow was Cort Chicago. Meg guessed he didn't really know the others yet. Cort felt he was winning. It showed in the way he squared up, looking down at Sam. A bully's pose, the stare, the tucked lip of a smile that was anything but.

"Mind your own business," Cort said to her, tossing it off with an insulting lilt. Sam hit him, barreling straight under to butt his head in that copious stomach, both fists scoring on the ribs. The big guy never guessed he was coming, staggered back, caught himself against the chair, lurched to one side, retched a few times and threw up. It smelled purely awful.

"Oh, Sam," Meg said. "I wish you hadn't done that."

Dilated pupils, rigors shook Sam, his clenched fists reddened with what would become bruises.

"What about coffee?" she said. For Sam, caffeine slowed him down, a paradoxical response, but she'd seen it before. Many spoonfuls heaped with sugar stirred into the black liquid, and no cream. She didn't touch Sam, just watched, her hand slightly lifted in his direction. He stared at it, so she held still.

Meg heard, half-saw someone bending down to talk to Cort on the ground, who exaggerated his sufferings with many groans and imprecations. Oh yes, that was Lincoln, comforting, safe; she could relax about that half of the event.

"Sam," she said again. "Like a cup of coffee?"

He felt like a vibrating line, a line wrapped around an animal, the animal panicked, holding for a moment before it breaks. Before it flails and falls in a tangle. White around his eyes.

"I'd like a cup," she said, taking a deep breath. "Will you come with me? It's been an overwhelming morning."

He jerked his head, and she took another slowing breath, turning towards the table, but not breaking eye contact, moving her fingers in an extension of welcome, an invitation, but without the threat of touching him.

◆ ◆ ◆

In spite of all Lincoln could say to Cort Chicago to calm him down, Cort called the cops. They talked with Sam, but he was back to looking so harmless that, in the end, Cort said forget it, because he could tell the cops were looking at the difference between the supposed aggressor and his victim and found it amusing that Sam was about half his size. Meg returned to her papers, trying to wrap her mind back around what she'd been doing before.

"Mrs. Meg, can we talk?"

Meg jumped. This time it was Officer Ray, and he had a look on his black face she simply couldn't figure out. Bad news? She didn't think so. But then he scowled as if he were practicing looking serious, so she didn't know what to think. She looked around the tables covered with bags of bread, plastic utensils and peanut butter jars under the awning. Thank the Lord it hadn't started to rain yet this fall, or they'd all be freezing. The homeless moved along, some casting glances at her and especially at Officer Ray.

"Bad news, but I don't think you should broadcast it. We found a pair of toes in the bushes at the park a week ago, but no certain ID. Female, that's about it; nothing like nail polish for a clue. Didn't find a lot of blood. I think it's reasonable to assume they're Jenny's toes, but the thing is, we've got no way to determine identity. Maybe she had some kind of accident and ran away. Something bad is going on in Isla Vista these days, and Goleta too. You told me some of your folk here been disappearing? That Winsome fellow? Got a bad feeling about it." He shook his head. "Other business, less scary. I have a little problem that could be a big one if it isn't handled right. You know that place with the fancy fish—koi—that some of the rich folk with gardens buy to put in ponds?"

"Yes?" she said.

"Come over here, will you?"

She walked some distance from the tables where the men and women were gathered, warming hands in worn mittens on their paper cups of coffee. Meg looked back. How tall and settled Dwayne looked these days. He hardly coughed any more. He saw her looking and gave her a wink that made her smile.

"You know how special some of those koi are at the Garden Center," Officer Ray said. "Worth a hundred thousand or more, they say. Well, we've been getting complaints that a couple disappeared. Big things." He made a gesture with his arms. "At the start it wasn't top expensive breeding stock that vanished, so they just let us know they had losses. I thought raccoons, but these fish are too big for raccoons, and the business has this electric fence to keep the critters out."

Why was he telling her this?

"A day ago I got another call. This time they're upset. They lost a huge monster fish, maybe this big, near two and a half feet long, with a special color of scales on him. It's the color and shine that made him rare."

"That's too bad," she said. "Do they have insurance? Can you insure fish?"

"Apparently when one's worth twenty thousand dollars, you can."

"Twenty thousand *dollars*?"

"Real special koi from some famous breeder in Japan, I'm told."

"What a strange story."

"And why am I telling you? Because I found something, heard something, and I need you to pass a message on. I heard Charlie telling Ilene about a good dinner they had together with Rapper. Barbecue. I discovered a long, stout fishing pole hidden in a clump of ceanothus bushes half a block from the Garden supply. Following that lead, I found a fire-pit and a batch of nice big fish bones, and Mrs. Meg, that was no ocean fish. I fish a bit myself when I get the chance, and I know."

"Twenty thousand dollars?"

"You bet. A twenty-thousand-dollar fish dinner. But it has to stop. I took the fishing pole, but I don't want to hear about even one more fish dinner. Make it so, Mrs. Meg."

She couldn't help it. Meg laughed so hard she cried. She tried to think about the poor fish. She tried to remind herself of the horror the owners must have felt. She tried really hard, but all she could do was laugh—laugh so hard she infected Officer Ray, who finally had to take off his glasses and blow his nose.

Her sides hurt when she finally stopped, more out of exhaustion than regained control.

"I swear," she said. "I will make sure there are no more fish dinners of this kind."

"You better." He put his glasses back on. "Oh, just asking, just wanted to make sure about what I said earlier; you really haven't seen Winsome?" He didn't show surprise when she shook her head. "Know where he holed up? Know his regular hides?"

"No. He had several places he talked about but he never said enough for me to be sure exactly where he meant. One he said gave him surf sounds to get him to sleep but that is a wide area to look through. I've been worried. Now I notice that Mr. Mock isn't around, and I thought he was going to stay the winter. He said the weather was so much better here than in Seattle. I'll give you a description of him, but let me catch my breath."

Looking past Officer Ray, she caught a sudden movement by the table. The new guy, who still hadn't given her his name, had been in line for coffee. Dwayne had seemed to shoulder him out, crowding him with his big frame. Then Dwayne looked across, caught her eye, and she saw he had a steadying hand on the stranger's grimy coat arm. For an instant, she hadn't known what she was seeing. Meg took a deep breath.

"OK, Officer. By the way, I'd like you to keep an eye on our new guy over here." She made a slight sideways jerk of her head to indicate whom she meant. "He still won't let me know his name."

"Yes," he said, "I've had an eye on him too."

◆ 27 ◆

Nicole stood on her rooftop sniffing the excitement rising from the streets of Isla Vista. Candy corn, crushed eucalyptus leaves, beer. For weeks the students had been laying plans. Halloween night tonight—police stood on all the roads into the coast town of Isla Vista, barricades with check points slowing traffic to a crawl into the university, whose borders blurred into the town. On a good year, the normal population of roughly 20,000 would triple. Thousands would manage to get in on the party, the streets would run with booze and vomit.

Nicole watched the people drift by. Still early, but the first costumes emerged. Wow, that was a glorious butterfly, wings swinging majestically, probably powered by batteries. The young woman between the wings gave an impression of nakedness, sure to gain that extra look. Those wings would get crushed when her costume made it onto El Embarcadero in a reeling press of bodies. The woman would be black and blue with pinch bruises. Nicole saw pirates' tri-corn hats headed down a street, then one of the apartment buildings opened its lobby doors, disgorging a clot of people whose costumes she couldn't make out, only that most seemed to be black. Vampires were all the rage—everyone looked thinner in black, didn't they?

She went back in the window. Maybe this year she'd go out, but she hesitated, looking at herself in the mirror. She would want a decent costume if she went. It would have been better to arrange a group, but which of her high school companions could she trust to keep their heads? Mom would let her go into the wild streets alone, if Nic wanted, but she wasn't in any mood to be groped by strangers. Would she ever be? Was that a taste that evolved with age? Nicole couldn't imagine being thrilled by the invasion of anonymous hands.

But that gave her an idea.

Later, when she went down to strut in front of Mom, Mom had to laugh.

"You're very handsome," she said. "Where did you get those shoulders?"

"I borrowed Dad's suit jacket. I'm going to roast because I have his cable sweater on under this, too."

She pulled her fedora over her eyes.

"A moustache would be too much?"

"That would make you look like a girl cross-dressing. Good job on the tie, Nic. All you need is a gambler's diamond ring, but you'll have to do without. Have fun, be careful, don't let anyone barf on Dad's jacket. You do have your cell?"

"You bet."

Nicole went out to the street, remembering to walk differently. Not that she normally did the hips and butt thing, but now she consciously strode with a male carelessness that felt good. Her pony tail itched a bit where she'd shoved it down the back of her shirt, but she'd worn worse. The year she'd wanted to be an amoeba had been the most uncomfortable of all—sitting had been impossible.

She wove her way in among the crowd.

◆ ◆ ◆

Nicole saw the bag man at the end of Pescadero. She stared with admiration and envy. Someone had cobbled together a disguise made entirely of plastic trash or shopping bags. No; second thought stopped her. Not envy. A costume entirely of plastic wouldn't breathe, the sweat would be streaming in no time. The person stood for the moment, stooping, alone at the end of the street.

Nicole looked about at the other masqueraders, an angel of indeterminate sex in sparkly tights, a crocodile with a flushed, drunken human face grinning out of the jaws, a horse costume that was surely down this alley in order to get out of the thickest part of the crowd. The owner of the horse was trying to duct-tape the rump back on—it had already been wrenched sideways, and no construction could withstand the stumbling raucous crowd next street over. The woman in riding breeches and pink riding jacket, her white stock already smeared with something like chocolate, helped him apply the tape; they must be a couple. So why did Nicole feel so alone when she looked back down to the end of the street at the plastic man? Was it the simple lack of eyes?

The creature made of garbage bags seemed to float towards her, eyeless, faceless. She decided she didn't like it, and Nicole believed in her own instincts. Familiar somehow, the way it stood, moved—made her feel as though she knew who the plastic bag man might be. Oh no. Dale, Dwayne, whatever his name was. The creepy guy Mrs. Meg liked. The turd who'd tried to steal her book.

She wanted nothing to do with him, but he seemed to be heading her way. With the caution of a cat, Nicole sidestepped down the alley, moving fast, back into the main crowds.

Nicole recalled Mom saying that anonymity made for bad behavior, and her own experience agreed. Better to go away when you felt that kind of unease. She'd never make the heroine of a horror movie. She looked back once and saw nothing in the alley but two couples making out. She averted her eyes fast. There were some things she didn't want to observe. If some day she wanted to do things like that, she wouldn't want to be out in public. Watching seemed even more embarrassing to her than it was for the participants.

Down another side street, between apartment buildings, further from the main press. Not too far, she knew she didn't want to end up isolated. Crowds at Halloween held danger but safety as well.

She glanced past the edge of one building, along the wall, movement catching her eye. What was that guy in the sequin costume doing with a plastic bag on his head? So peculiar. He slumped against the wall, sliding down to his knees, the bag billowing, seeming to stretch bigger.

"What are you doing out alone, missy?"

She jumped, looking over her shoulder. Plastic bag man. Yes, that was Dwayne again, closer than she ever wanted him to get. She took a fast step aside and sprinted away. Maybe she hadn't got a letter in track, but by the end of this year, she was going to think about it.

◆ ◆ ◆

About an hour later, Nicole had seen as much as she could take for one Halloween. She'd only been pinched once, and the man who did it had obviously taken her for another male. His apologies, when she turned and confronted him, made her erupt in giggles as soon as she managed to get far enough away that he wouldn't likely see. But he'd been under the influence, so she probably could have laughed in his face, and he'd never remember.

Crossing Del Playa, she felt she'd left her departure a little on the late side. The tenor of the crowd had changed to both more relaxed and more aggressive. She had to push herself between people, too much contact for comfort, and she hoped Dad's jacket wasn't going to show some horrid anonymous smear when she got home. Yes, later than she ought. She heard the unmistakable spatter of someone throwing up. Yuck. Nicole pried herself out from the press of the crowd, all the smells of perfume, perspiration and alcohol, the sweet waft of candy and melting chocolate combining with incense from the nearby apartment building with jack o'lanterns in the windows. Smoky pumpkin and a mixed reek of humanity.

There are too many of us. Ripe for the picking. She looked up at the stars dimmed by all the lights here below. Humans were ready prey for some new predator to come along. What you can't see can come and get you. She'd definitely stayed out too long. She'd been careful enough not to eat or drink anything, even all the free goodies proffered with smiles and good wishes, but she felt now like she'd eaten too big a meal of sticky things. Yuck.

Nicole passed the police cordon, moving through different groups. She saw another man, or maybe it wasn't a man, leaning against the Rainbow Apartment wall as though he were trying to recollect himself. Probably exactly what was wrong with him. Uncollected self. It was only when she turned down Sabado and took a deep breath of relief, finally finding herself in a quieter zone with couples strolling by, that she had a sudden annoyed feeling as if someone were staring.

Her first ploy for problems of unwanted attention was to look at her wrist as if she had a watch, and walk on fast, acting the role of *late for an appointment*. It didn't work. She still felt eyes focused on her. She would have to find a way to look back. She shouldn't feel so pursued when the streets were filled. It wasn't as though she were here alone. There must be forty others walking with her in the street on this block.

Crossing the street, she managed to look back, and dread rose like a lump in her throat when she saw a plastic draped figure among the other costumed shapes. Shopping bag costume of translucent plastic, black and brown. Moving with that gravity-defying drift; Dwayne must have practiced that with some sick sense of humor.

What were the odds? She calculated them. She never played the lottery. She didn't believe there was a plan for her written in the stars. But she also had a belief in predator/prey relationships, and she wanted out. She sped up, trying not to look obvious. She felt her hands sweat inside the gloves she wore, the prickle of her hair down her collar.

Dodging another inebriated couple, she bumped into someone tall who caught her by the shoulder. She rebounded, ready to counterattack, balanced on her feet the way she'd learned in judo, and looked up.

"Steady," said Jack Kushner.

◆ ◆ ◆

She planned a sidestep to pass around him, taking another fast look over her shoulder. *Transparent, idiot; now Dwayne will know you know he's following you.*

"Nicole?" Jack didn't waste time on surprise, wrapped his cloak around himself. "You're not OK," he said. "I'll walk with you. Someone bothering you?"

"Hurry," she said.

He did, and his stride was good—long, loose, and fast.

"Who is it? Some punk from school?"

"Don't know," she said, more honest than she wanted to be. "It's the garbage bag man. Did you see him?"

"What?"

She was glad to see he didn't do anything so obvious as look back. "No, I don't mean a guy who picks up the garbage. A nasty piece of work I know, costumed in plastic shopping bags."

"I've seen several tonight," he said. "Interesting."

"What?" she said, a little breathless. She would have to look back in another moment. She hunched her shoulders in Dad's coat and imagined a plastic touch brushing weightless against her. In just a moment, it would happen. It shouldn't matter, but it did.

"Interesting that you don't believe anyone's going to help you out," he said. "You're moving through the crowd. You passed a policeman on a horse and didn't even look twice, so I've got to be wrong."

"Wrong?"

"I imagined maybe you turned in some drug runners or something like that, and that's why you don't depend on people to give you a hand. You don't think being in public will make whoever's bothering you back off."

He managed all these long pronouncements without any apparent lack of breath, though hers was coming fast and a little tight. She kept remembering the sequined man in the alley with a shopping bag over his head. Not funny. There was something very bad about that memory but she couldn't tease it out. Maybe she should have checked if the sequined man were all right.

"You're sweating."

"That's not a polite thing to say," Nicole said, trying to laugh. It stuck in her throat.

She looked back. Dwayne wasn't visible; instead, she saw a shopping bag drifting between feet, seeming strangely purposeful. Garbage, trash, but why did it seem that an empty discarded piece of litter moved like a jellyfish in water, as though it intended something?

"You're wearing a suit and tie, so the usual courtesies due a lady go by the way." Jack said.

A drop hit her cheek. "It's raining," she said. "I mean, it's not that I'm not sweating, but look. That isn't fair, not on Halloween."

"I thought it never rains in Southern California."

"Rains in season. Like monsoons. This is early. I think you'd do better to turn off here and go another way. I'm headed home. I don't think Dwayne will bother you if you're not with me."

Single drops, widely spaced. The heat of the crowd would evaporate them on Del Playa. No one would even notice. She could still see a few stars overhead between tattered clouds. This wasn't a real storm, only some passing shower.

"Curiouser and curiouser," he said. "By the way, I hate Lewis Carroll."

"That pedophile." She ducked around a moving castle with three pairs of feet. They caught up with each other on the far side of the castle. "Poor stupid Alice, but her parents were worse. Do you mind if I start running?"

"Depends what it is you want me to do. Make a last valiant stand behind you and lay the villains low, though I don't know who they are, or run, too?"

"Run, too," she said. "But maybe not the same direction."

"Huh," he said, "I'll stick with you to see what's next."

She flashed one more irresistible glance behind before she took off and stumbled down into a long, sliding fall on hands and knees in candy wrappers, gum and spit. She swore, adding extra details when Jack hauled her up by one arm. Thank God she'd chosen to wear gloves, and Dad's coat escaped damage.

"I don't see anyone following," he said. "Take a breath."

"Yes," she said. She stared back, peering around the costumes and partiers. "Stop; look. I don't know. He's gone."

She didn't want to tell the odd idea she'd had about the shopping bag.

"Could he be taking another route? Cutting us off?"

"Then he'd have to know where I live." She stared about, trying to catch any possible clue. A white shopping bag eddied past, catching on the boot of the Lone Ranger. No more plastic bag man, though.

"You realize what the pursuit implies?"

She looked at him, noticing that indeed Jack took this seriously. His eyes kept moving, scanning for garbage men, his mouth set tight. He seemed white to her, but it could be the lighting.

"You're not crazy. He isn't following just anyone. It's you. But I think he's a coward, because he's not in sight now. Think it's simply because there are two of us?"

She caught her breath. They had left the main crowds behind. He kept to her pace, striding past the apartment complexes. Every so often someone passed them, headed to the party. A fellow in a black crow suit flapped once at them in apparent camaraderie and cawed before continuing on his way.

"I appreciate your company," she said to Jack. "Thank you."

"Bet that hurt to say," he said, "but I will, like the gentleman I am, see you to your door, unless you're worried about my knowing where you live. I promise you I don't talk to trash bags."

"Glad to know you try to keep good company," she said, but now all of a sudden she felt her knees shaking. Talk, damn it, she ordered herself. Make it seem as normal as possible to be running from a particular costume on a Halloween evening. Sure, everyone had enemies.

"I don't know why I got so spooked," she said. "It was one of those instinctive things. I hate things without faces."

"Mean of you to start backing off on telling about this threatening guy. Best if what you know, I know that you know," he said. "You could come clean."

"I'm linear, and I'm honest," she said. "If you never learn anything else about me, you'll have to accept that. Good night, Mister Kushner."

She made him a formal bow, turned up the flagstones, and went fast to the door. He'd already started back the way they'd come when she opened it. Nicole hesitated a long moment; a few drops of rain sprinkled the stoop and her shoulders. No garbage bags. No plastic shopping bags. Nothing but the small sounds of scattered rain like tiny feet in the trees and bushes. She shivered and went in.

◆ 28 ◆

"Dad, I really need you to have another look at my science project. I have strange DNA, except it's not DNA, it's XNA. Remember when we discussed how aliens might work out reproduction differently? The other night when we were talking?"

"Clever, Nic. Good try. I am not putting you on the list of proposals for my extraterrestrial biology grant committee."

"Dad, I need help on this. Sam thinks I'm mucking around with my results because I think it's funny. He's threatening to stop me from using the PCR machine. He didn't want to get me in trouble with you, so he said he would let me do one more run."

"Are you giving my graduate student grief?"

She couldn't say no, but it wasn't the kind of problem Dad thought. Looking up at his narrow, laughter-lined face, she realized how much real sympathy hid behind his spectacles. If he could pause, take measure of what was important, they would all be OK.

"Look Nic, I really don't have time. I'm putting you off for good reason, but you know I can't just cancel every obligation because you think you found alien DNA in Freedom Park."

"Or because I've seen aliens?"

"Looking like?"

"Those plastic garbage bags you get from K-Mart."

Dad laughed.

"I love it. That will get on the *Santa Barbara News Distress* front page for sure, especially if you time the release of the announcement with the debate on outlawing those menaces. Oh hell, there's my taxi. Give Mom my love. I'm going to miss you guys. Tell her next time I want her to take me to the airport, so I can leave as late as possible."

He gave her a quick peck on the top of her head then swept out the door. Another thing gone all wrong. Mom had never failed to take him to the airport before.

Nicole waved him off in the yellow cab, its headlights racing across the yard, shortening against the bushes, lengthening again, then blocked by the vehicle's low body. The cab sped away from where she stood in the doorway.

A cold night, a regular night, but she felt ready to kill something. There was Dad going off lonely, neglected. It hurt her so much she wanted to cry, even though she wasn't the kind of person who did the pitiful. She missed him, felt like the house was broken by his leaving.

Then she focused on her fury that what she had said in all seriousness, he hadn't heard. Sounded funny, of course it did. Plastic bags. She had blown it, perhaps on purpose, because she didn't know what she wanted. To make him stay, like some child who says "Daddy, I'm sick" when her father has to go away on business? How could she convey conviction when she didn't know if she wanted him to believe her? Not yet. If she could figure this puzzle out and then show him, that would be worth pride.

He'd laughed, but she felt real horror envisioning how the plastic bags might surge after her, then drift, moving with alternate speed and deliberation as though they swam like jellyfish in the ocean of air. The picture made her shudder, standing cold. The sound of her father's taxi faded down the streets of the town. She found herself wishing she'd finished reading *It*, as if Stephen King might have a clue how to cross the bridge of belief. Wasn't one of his themes disbelief, the tendency that everyone had to erase the extraordinary? Even memories of good things. Especially adults.

She looked up into a night sky of stars and remembered the meteorite that she'd seen flare into purple and knew that extremes got taken down. Beautiful and horrible things tended to get erased, forgotten because of the needs of ordinary, boring, mundane things of the world. That was worth crying about.

Rage, rage against the dying of the light. She would defy all the erasures. She would rage. She would remember, think, and figure out, because out there, by day and by night, she at least, knew something was coming.

◆ 29 ◆

Meg had finally found time in the late afternoon to write her order for new breakfast supplies when someone tapped on the propped-open door of the trailer. She looked up and saw the strawberry blond hair of her visitor. Dread shrank her stomach. It had been such a nice day until now.

"Meg." Karen stepped up at her invitation, carefully closing the door behind her, without asking. "I wanted to follow up on our earlier discussion. Things have been so busy that I haven't had any time until now."

"Yes?" Meg said, polite and wary.

"You know that our congregation is disturbed by your male visitor. We want to trust you, but the flesh is weak. Meg, your example stands before us all, our children, our youth. I've asked Father to come to talk with you. He should be here any moment."

"Do you wish to sit down?" Meg said, making an effort.

"Thank you," Karen said. A rap on the door brought Meg to open it for Father Stephens, who, in his sober suit, with the kindly look behind his thick glasses, gave her his customary warm smile. Even Karen seemed to sit a little bit more relaxed after he pulled up his chair.

Karen spoke first, saying much what she'd said the first time, but this time Meg detected a threat that she'd not faced before.

"I'm not sure, Father, that Meg should be working for the church when she is living in suspicious circumstances. Think of the message our church strives to give, a message of consistency and faith that is so much denigrated by outside influences in the media and the world. In the outside world, anything goes. No one cares for the appearance of sin. But we, as a church, must."

"So, what do you have to tell me, Meg?" Father Stephens pushed his heavy glasses back up his stubby nose and blinked.

"It's a question of charity, Father," Meg said. "I happened to be the person who was free to give Dwayne a ride back to Isla Vista the day the hospital decided to release him. He shouldn't have been released. I fault them for that. They'd given him antibiotics, rehydrated him, and stopped the progress of his pneumonia, but he was still gravely ill and very weak. I couldn't drop him off at Freedom Park and drive away feeling like I'd done my duty."

"I see."

"Wasn't there an option of a Rehabilitation Center?" Karen said.

"If there was, no one at the hospital told me."

"I looked into this, Father. They did offer it to Mr. Wallace, but he refused. Of his own free will, apparently expressing himself in an abusive manner to the social worker. He said he'd made arrangements. Even so, the social worker made sure he had a friend coming to pick him up. As for his future accommodations, either he and Meg had already agreed to cohabit, or he lied."

Meg felt her face flush. "I had no agreement with him, and I object to the word *cohabit*, which implies an intimacy I allow no one."

"This seems to be water under the bridge, Karen," Father Stephens said. "I think the problem is a little different, and it hinges on that word, different. Meg, how is this man different from the others you serve in your position?"

"He is my answer to the old question—*how then, shall we live*? He was the one by my path at a time that I could help."

Father Stephens nodded.

"How long do you foresee that he will be your guest?"

"I don't know. Winter is a cruel time."

"For all of them. He does have a vehicle?"

"Yes, he does," Meg said. She felt as if something more was being lost than this argument. "Father, I have done no wrong with this man, and I hold as truly as any other member of our congregation by the truth of the Testaments. You would be the first human being that I would come to if I had sin on my conscience. Are there not other arguments to be made?"

"Such as?"

"An example of charity? If I can open my garage to a needy man, what could my neighbors in the congregation do?"

"Some of us have children to shield," Karen said.

"I do not. But I do have other roommates, plus two dogs for my protection."

Father Stephens considered her for a long minute before he nodded to Karen.

"Meg," Karen said, her anxiety making her more appealing than she'd ever seemed before to Meg, "Do you truly believe that what you do is right?"

"With all my heart."

"Then as your sister in Christ, I will accept that," she said. "For now. But be careful Meg. The Devil has many traps, and he sets the greatest number concealed as good deeds."

Father Stephens remained after Karen embraced Meg and left. "I hope you hold no resentment?" he said.

"She has my welfare at heart," Meg said. "I didn't think so the first time we spoke."

"Meg, do you feel an attraction to this man Dwayne?"

She looked down at her plump hands, not wanting to meet his eyes then.

"Yes," she said. "But it's not driving what I do. This is truly, Father, a simple small thing I could do for someone whom I hoped to help. He is not for me."

"Remember that then. I note he has made no gesture to approach our services or our congregation, and while that could be an honorable choice of a man who doesn't want to seem overeager to move into your life, you must always remember, he is not your brother in the church. Your spiritual life must always come first. There is no inequality like that between a person of faith and one who has none, shackled together in an intimate relation."

"I shall remember," she said. Father Stephens rose to leave. "Thank you so much for listening, for understanding."

Meg resettled herself in her chair more comfortably and tried to return to ordering cases of peanut butter from Costco, but what she recalled was Dwayne. His touches, the gestures, the elements of interaction that so genteelly spoke of the romantic tension she felt between them. She was not alone in feeling this. Did she believe what she had said, that Dwayne was not for her?

◆ ◆ ◆

"Meg." Lincoln put his well-meaning, pimply face against the open door.

Not now, Lincoln; Meg suppressed a sigh. Was she ever going to get anything done today?

"It's Charlie. He's crying," Lincoln said.

Was Officer Ray right—did Charlie have something on his conscience? No, she was never going to believe Charlie could have hurt Jennie. He had a soft spot a mile wide; just look at his dog following him adoringly everywhere. But she had better go see if he was all right.

"Hey, Charlie," she said, sitting down on the log by the sycamore he leaned against. "You OK?"

Of course he wasn't. She could hear his breathing rough and

thick, see the silver reflection of tears on his skin that caught sunlight from the partially clouded sky. His short blond hair fell about his face and the scarred hand he pressed across his eyes. Wonder what made those scars, maybe burns? He jerked a nod, so she sat quiet, waiting. Boister whined, pressed in against his foot. It felt like a long time to Meg. The log was making her left foot go to sleep.

She saw Rapper hop his bike and go trundling off, his huge duffel on his back like he was a turtle. Sometimes he hung out with Charlie, but not today, she guessed. Maybe some hard words had passed.

"You have some trouble, Charlie?" she said. Boister came over to sniff her hand hopefully, but she didn't have any Milk Bones for him today.

"Got Rapper pissed because I'm too sensitive," Charlie said. "Says I'm so soft it makes him sick sometimes. Today is sometimes."

"We all get sad," Meg said.

"I think too much. Need a switch to turn off."

"Yeah. I wish I had one too."

"Thinking about Jenny, so sad. Disappeared like that, then I took her stuff. It's like she never came here, like no one ever knew her. She just up and gone."

"You have any idea at all what might have happened to her?"

"There at night, gone by morning. Boister didn't bark."

"So do you think there was any way someone might have hurt her?"

"Dunno. She was nice. Quiet. Scared all the time. Didn't bother anyone. Didn't have much. I heard some guy robbed her, week before, so who'd a done her, for her stuff? She had nothing really good left. I know she kinda hung around me because of Boister. Figured the dog would bark for her if a bad thing happened. She liked him. Gave him scraps. We miss her. I'm the only guy who got anything from her being gone."

Surely no one would talk like that if he'd been the killer. Meg felt sure Charlie was innocent of Jenny's disappearance.

"If I up and go, if I disappear, Mrs. Meg, will you take my dog? Boister's a good dog. Rapper says he can't care for a dog."

Meg had to agree. Rapper was one who simply went "off" at intervals; couldn't even talk when he was in one of his fits.

"Don't worry. If I'm here, I will," she said. "We can set it up."

Who knew what Popeye and Perry would think, but she'd deal with that, when or if the day came. "But I think you're gonna be fine, Charlie. You'll find some work, get a place."

"Left Nevada two years back. Got taken for drunk up in SLO; don't know why I went there, but I kept thinking about my wife with that guy she picked up. I think they're in Nevada. I wanted out so they wouldn't know I was drinking. Didn't want they should tell the kids the old man's a drunk. She got a good man this time, he wouldn't make up shit about me, but he wouldn't hide it, neither."

"Sounds like I'd need a better friend than that; just saying," Meg said. Her foot hurt, tingled, but if she moved, Charlie might think she was bored or uncomfortable to be talking with him. "Don't think I'm perfect enough for the likes of him."

"Perfect enough," said Charlie. "If I were Rapper, could write a song about you, I could."

In that moment, Meg felt as though she were an alien, stepping into an expectation she had no frame for, no way to appreciate. She knew he meant it as a gift, as a compliment, but it felt like being given an armadillo—she had no idea how to feed it or how she ought to say thank you.

"See this?" He bared his teeth, set a fingertip against his center left incisor. "Got that chipped in Sonoma by a hot tempered dude. Spent the night in jail, cause the cops didn't understand he hit me first. That's what killed that tooth. See, if it has a dark line at the gums or if it looks kinda see-through, grayish, you know it's dead."

"Good to know," Meg said. She noted Rapper returning, all his stuff on his back as before, but carrying a paper bag. His brakes squealed as he stopped.

"Yeah. But I bet all your teeth are great. You have a nice smile, Mrs. Meg."

"Hey," Rapper sauntered up, but in spite of the casual way he slouched, Meg looked at the wax paper shape in his hand and couldn't keep from smiling.

"Charlie, gotta coupon two-for-one at Subway," Rapper said. "Thought you could use a bite. It's turkey and provolone with all the veggie stuff and mayo."

Charlie sat up and looked past Meg at Rapper.

"Thank you. You the man, Rapper," Charlie said. "Thank you. Thank you."

"Shut up already," Rapper said. "Eat your goddamn sand-wich. Go on."

◈ 30 ◈

Brian swung around the corner.

What bothered him? He poked about in his mind until he pinned it down. It was that flapping plastic bag at the Addison's pool Wednesday. He'd had a big box for them so he had to drive his truck. He'd gone up to the door balancing their package in his arms, sur-prised to see Julie Addison waiting for him, swinging her door open.

"It's a present for John," she said. "I only hope he's not too pissed about my getting it, but what's a credit card for?"

Talking too much, but at least this time she had clothes on. He steered around the white couch, straight to the coffee table before he set it down. Fragile. Mrs. Addison, you're lucky I care.

"Hey, Mrs. Addison."

An unfamiliar male voice, pool guy out there, cap pulled back on his head, his t-shirt and shorts showing the traditional tanned physique of a man who spent hours brushing down algae. Brian made sure the package wasn't going to slide, then looked at the glass back door that led onto the poolside. Back drive separated from pool by a reed fence. Too small a lot, for both things. Looked tatty. Looked pretentious without the space to carry it off.

"Ma'am? You need to order more acid," the pool guy said. "Your pool runs basic."

"Is it a problem?" Julie Addison said, leaving Brian. He could see his usefulness was over.

"All pools in the area run basic," the pool guy said. "It's just the way the water is. But it plays heck with the chlorine, so I need to get you to sign off on some more. I'll bring the stuff by tomor-row to treat the pool. It's running near eight on PH."

Brian dusted his hands, his attention caught on a funny move-ment by the turquoise pool. What was that? A grocery bag, one of those ugly tan ones, half-inflated. Blowing over the pool surface toward that sparrow perched on the edge of the tiles.

Weird. Wasn't the wind from west to east this afternoon? That was a fast moving bag. He checked against the trees, glanced over at the pool guy holding out his forms for Mrs. Addison to sign. Looked back, now the bag was on the edge. Must have scared the bird off. But it seemed like that bag was clinging to the edge of the pool, pulling itself up over the verge. In fact, it wasn't touching the water any more. Brian blinked, became aware of Mrs. Addison's stare.

"Thank you," she said. Pointedly.

"You're welcome, ma'am." he said. He left.

Guess his eyes were growing old. Or a warp in the glass. Sometimes panes of glass didn't come out right and made you see crooked, depending on the angle. Go see the eye doctor, maybe. But it all felt wrong.

◆ 31 ◆

Something moved. Mariette stopped, her hands clamped on the bitter cold metal of the dumpster's rolled edge. She jerked her head back, left, right, scanning. Godamercy, how she missed having glasses. Everything doubled, fuzzed in the dim, blocked from the sodium lights' false cheer here by the loading dock. They said past forty, your eyes started getting better, but she hadn't the luck.

Maybe a rat. She hated rats. A shudder brought more cold air in down her sweater collar. Right there on the far edge of the dumpster. Rat. Skittery, scratchy, with those bead eyes that looked like they'd been glued on. Not like a nice animal with real eyelids. Did rats have eyelids? She remembered the spotted rat in elementary school, Mrs. Klimpt's class. Never saw it sleep; it always burrowed down in the newspaper like it didn't trust anyone. She thought she saw a rat, now, in that gray shape hunched on the edge of a box.

What would Mrs. Klimpt say if she could see Mariette Hughes now?

"Has Mrs. Klimpt died, rat?" She had gray hair back then, when Mariette sat in her fourth grade classroom. Probably watching her from heaven right now. Mariette turned her head to peer over the rigid icy metal rim of the dumpster.

"Did you leave me anything good, rat? A packet of stale candy bars or a crushed box of cereal would be great. Or out-of-date cheese." Oh, that would be so good. Her mouth filled with saliva at the thought of salty, oily cheese. Mrs. Klimpt thought Mariette the smartest in her class. "Look down and see me be smart, feeling through the garbage on a Monday night, Mrs. Klimpt.

"I try to keep myself proper, but I can't see well, so I have to grab at lots of stuff I don't want to touch," she said to the rat and Mrs. Klimpt. "Are you my guardian angel? You the one that made the late-night checker forget to lock the dumpster down the way he's supposed to? I promise, I'll make it look good and neat before I'm gone, unless a cop comes along. Got to hurry; thank you, Mrs. Klimpt."

For a moment she hung there, not wanting to move. The metal radiated cold against her layers of sweater and jacket, through her pants and the tights underneath. She knew she'd get wet once she started pawing around, and it would burn like ice and sog her clothes with stink.

Think, girl; move it. Lucky no one else was here. Hurry. She looked back, thought she saw the drift of movement like a shadow between her and the lights of the parking lot. A ghost. No, if she thought about angels it would *be* an angel. Mrs. Klimpt. Something nice.

She wasn't going to think about how Mrs. Klimpt's breath always stank of used coffee and cigarettes so that little Mariette held her breath, how the teacher's body moved stiff as cardboard under her frumpy dress. Dresses of windowpane plaid, or little bouquets of flowers, polkadots. Mrs. Klimpt approved of Mariette, there'd been kindness along with the rank breath, a motion with her hand as if she might have patted Mariette's shoulder. Think good thoughts and move, girl. Don't piss off the ghosts—no, sorry, never thought that word *piss* either. Mariette hooked an elbow over the edge and heaved herself up.

A whooshing sort of noise, a blur of gray rose up around her, expanding, blinding her. No air. Agony seared her eyeballs before she could see nothing, pain ripping her skin, her face, lips, followed by the unending fall.

◆ 32 ◆

Dad went off to Washington again, so reluctant he seemed to leave a furrow behind him. Reassuring to see how much he didn't want to leave. Even though Nicole knew he hated asking other professors to cover his classes, it seemed to her his distaste for going grew.

Jack Kushner avoided saying anything to Nicole in class or out of it. Worst of all, Nicole ran out of good books to read. She wanted horror in the dark of the year and besides, when things sucked, she always felt better when she read stories about people who had it a lot worse. So she was delighted to find a battered old paperback by H.P. Lovecraft on her bed in the early afternoon on Friday when the world had already turned gray before its time.

She dropped all her stuff on the floor and sat down to read. Sometime deep in the *Mountains of Madness* she switched on the lamp so she could see the pages, but by the time she smelled dinner, she'd finished the book. A shame she could read so fast. She went down the hall toward the kitchen, the book in her arm the way she used to carry favorite stuffed toys, like her green fluffy giant microbe that represented the Flu. Wonder where she'd put that old thing.

Her mother whipped up a sauce. She could tell by the preoccupation on Mom's face that only half of Mom's brain attended to the stir fry that sizzled and spat in her pan. It had chicken and peapods with red peppers. Nicole hated red peppers. Slimy. She only liked hot chilies, not these slimy sweetish things, but now wasn't a time to bitch.

"Mom," she said. "Thank you for the *Mountains of Madness*. That was a great read."

"You don't mind his language, then?" Mom turned with her glasses fogged from the heat of cooking, or maybe from steam rising from the pot of rice on the back of the stove.

"Love it. Makes me slow down and pay attention, then I start trying to pronounce the unpronounceable names like Cthulhu or Yog Sthoth or something like that."

"Yog Sothoth. Yes, and Shub-Niggurath, the Goat with a Thousand Young. Too bad you finished so fast."

"Exactly what I was thinking. Pity they're no track contests in reading. I'd get a varsity letter."

"Dinner in five."

"I'll wash. Tomorrow, can I cook?"

They ate quickly. Nicole noticed that Mom plied her chopsticks as if with other things than food on her mind. All her worries about her parents surged up, and Nicole's appetite deserted her.

"Is everything all right, Mom?"

"You keep asking me that as though I were sick or something."

"Sorry. I miss Dad."

"So do I, but it makes a good time to get ahead in work, and that's what I'm thinking about."

Not as reassuring as she might like, but then again, Mom was so linear. Nicole went back to using her chopsticks to shovel food as efficiently as possible into her mouth. Peasant manners but Mom didn't look critical right now, and, speaking of mountains, Nicole had a mountain of work to do after indulging her read-fest. She washed up the dishes fast, then headed for her room and schoolbooks.

Near nine o'clock, the doorbell rang. Nicole jerked alert from her advanced algebra, first puzzled, then alarmed. Who would be here at this hour? Bad news? Was something wrong with Dad? She found herself looking around her small room with its gold-patterned Indian bedspread, the creamy white pillowcases, the tall packed bookcases with all the stories she had read and loved waiting there for her return to the countries and people she imagined. Could simply being here stop bad news? Maybe you could do magic. Maybe there was a rewind button for life, or even a pause so you could stay in a good place. The trick was knowing when you wanted to hit the button. She guessed she'd waited too long. She heard Mom's voice at the door, sprang up as though she could put herself between Mom and change.

"Nic. You have a visitor." Mom had the faintest note of question in her voice. Nicole loved her for not doing the embarrassing question and answer routine that normal parents surely would have done.

"Jack?" she said in her turn, more surprise than seemed polite showing, she was sure.

He came in straightening his shoulders, maybe not certain if he should put his hands in his pockets, but all in all, looking as if he came to be friends. Nicole found herself smiling. This was awkward. What was he here for, and why now?

Good manners have a place. They give you things to say and do when someone forgot to give you the script.

"Mom, this is Jack Kushner, a newcomer to the high school. Jack, this is my mother, Professor Lee Carlquist."

"I know your parents," Mom said. "They work down the hall from my lab."

Handshaking, polite necessaries.

"Your mother isn't the curious type," he said when they went into the living room.

"You underestimate her. She sure is, but she's not an eavesdropper. She doesn't approach my friends with an oyster knife."

"What do you know about oyster knives?"

"Enough. Mom comes from New England. If she wants to know something she'll ask you, not play around."

Jack stood there in the living room as if she hadn't gestured at the chairs, hands in his thrift store jacket pockets, a little slouched as seemed to be normal for boys who were taller than they wanted to be. He wasn't bad looking, only unfinished, if you compared him to Sam in Dad's lab. Ten years younger, too, she supposed. He seemed to be noting the things that interested him—it showed good sense that what he chose were shelves of books, then odd bits of stone and wood on the coffee table, which had never had coffee set on it.

"I need to know what we're doing for this science project," he said. "I promise I won't screw it up."

"Do you really care?" she said. "If you leave me alone, I'll get it done, and I'll let you paste down the print-outs on the science project cardboard presenter Mr. Marks approves. Black or white backgrounds only. Three panels. Not much to choose."

"Do you have any idea why I'm here? Why my dad ended up taking the job at this institution?"

"You make it sound like 'mental' is supposed to precede institution. UCSB's a good university even if it has the bad luck to be sitting on the beach in Santa Barbara."

"That's as it may be."

"God, you do sound like a New Englander."

"I was. Look, let me get this over with. Dad got a great offer from the Engineering Department at UCSB, but it's not the only reason we moved."

"You killed someone? Witnessed a crime and had to be relocated?"

"Shut up already. I blew up the chemistry lab."

"No."

"Yes."

"How? Prove it."

"Go look at the papers online," he said. "I left the Bunsen Burner on when working after hours. Unlit. We're all lucky the spark was an automatic timer switching on the thermostat in the night when the place was empty, or we'd be talking murder."

"Involuntary manslaughter is what they'd call it," Nicole said, sitting up. "You know what, I don't believe you. You're shitting me."

"I wouldn't shit you. You're my favorite turd."

"You're a sullen, self-righteous bastard, but you wouldn't be that dumb. I've been watching you, and you have no habits of the recently-afflicted-with-OCD-because-of-a-life-event. You're OCD because you were *born* that way. It's in your genes."

"Do you always talk this way?"

"Yes. Why do you think all my friends are nerds, and even they find me a bit much to take on a long day?"

He sat down. Mom tapped on the doorframe of the living room to alert them she was there.

"If you two can get along well enough, there are some cookies on the cooling rack. I'm in the study if you need anything." She nodded at them both and went back off down the hallway.

"Were we that loud?" Nicole said, embarrassed.

"I don't think your mom needed her oyster knife tonight," Jack said. "Now that we've established that I'm a liar with terminal OCD, how about those cookies, while you tell me what we're doing for the science project? What kind are they? The cookies, I mean."

"Snickerdoodles. Cinnamon sugar..."

"Oh, yes. New England as heck. Want. Now, please."

The cookies had hit that perfect temperature where they wouldn't burn your mouth but still had a soft heat in the middle under the crunch of cinnamon sugar. When he nodded at the raised carton and her questioning look, she poured them each a glass of milk. Back in the living room, he finished off his second cookie before he spoke.

"So what's your plastic bag phobia about?"

"Aside from the plastic trash issue? Animals getting strangled and that sort of thing," she said, suddenly wanting to take a risk. If he couldn't be trusted, was it better to know now? "I don't like the way they move. Sometimes against the wind."

"Like Halloween night," he nodded. "Could be eddies."

"Creeps me out."

"Yeah."

"Halloween night, I saw a guy in the alley with one over his face. He was leaning against the wall like he was stinking drunk. That man you saw following me startled me away. But I can't stop thinking about the guy in the alley. It looked wrong somehow."

"Analyze," Jack said, starting on his third cookie. "What was wrong? Examine the image."

"Shorter than you are. He wore a sequined suit; it caught the light from the street behind me."

"And I don't look good in sequins."

"Sagging, so he slid down the wall, bag moving down over head and neck."

"No one else there?"

"Couldn't see anyone else near him. But it was fairly dark."

"You said the bag moved? He was pulling it down?"

"No."

Nic stopped and looked at her cookie.

"I could have sworn that bag was moving down, starting to cover his shoulders—that's a really big bag, isn't it? But his arms hung down at his sides."

"Now, that's creepy."

"Don't make fun of me," Nicole said.

"I'm not. Just saying that maybe your stalker has more to do with your dislike of plastic bags than you've considered. Coming up behind you trying to spook you, maybe he succeeded."

❖ 33 ❖

"I really want to go, so let's not be late," Julie Addison said, opening the back door wide onto the bright autumn evening. Long clouds of salmon and pink arced across the violet sky. She felt the energy of anticipation, adjusted the earring in her right ear so that the diamonds would match the angle of the left ones. Nothing like knowing how good you look.

She turned back, leaving the door open.

"James? Where are you?"

She walked back into the cool house, enjoying the crisp click of her elegant heels on the linoleum. Some day when James got a really big raise, she'd get carpet. Even in the kitchen. Who cooked these days, anyway? But maybe people would think that was odd. Maybe a bit of ceramic tile for the kitchen would help if James spilled the coffee in the morning. Tile wouldn't be too expensive to get clean. Imagine the dining room and hallway, though; good sculpted Berber wool would make a great setting for her. She glanced around at the pale walls. Silver touches here and there, mirrors making the rooms seem bigger than they really were. Yes, a new high-quality carpet that extended through the whole house would give the right opulent impression. But maybe they should get a new house, in some better part of town.

Now, James was dragging his heels about going to the Wessex Bank Fundraiser. If he wanted a promotion, he needed to tend the social image. She went back down the hall.

"I'm ready," she said, pitching it soft and sweet. "You wearing the brown suit tonight, babe? I'm in my new taupe, so don't wear gray."

She heard him say something, but she dashed into the bathroom to touch up the little smudge on her lipstick. This was a new color, with a slight iridescence like her mother-of-pearl buttons. Done, she popped her head out the bathroom door and saw him adjusting his tie, a slight smile, even if a tired one, on his handsome face. She loved blonds, surfer dude good looks, and he fit the bill. Who would guess it was hours at the Hawaii Tanning salon rather than on the waves that gave him the healthy color of an athlete?

"You look great, sexy," she said and saw his smile deepen. A little kindness and men responded, especially if you looked the way she did. Anyway, he was a sweetie.

She let him lead back toward the living room and kitchen. She hadn't meant to spend quite so long in the bathroom, and the wind had kicked up. Disgusting, a plastic shopping bag, someone else's trash, had blown in the door. She saw James bend to pick it up but he staggered, knelt, fell down on the linoleum with a gargling sound. Julie's first thought was heart attack—but he'd been fine seconds ago, it wasn't possible. Then she saw what was happening and opened her mouth to scream. No sound came out but a dry squeak.

James's face had stretched into a mask of silent pain, his arms buried in the blousing, flaring shape of the shopping bag, whose gelatinous sides seemed to pump in and out. It stretched, embracing his nice suit and chest, then down to his hips and thighs. The sides thinned so she could see through. The brown of his suit faded, shredding away, the exposed white of his shirt flared bright red. A flush of blood, quickly paling into pink, the rosy hues of muscle and white of bone, some other colors of rounded shapes inside him she didn't know by name, all swirling inside the glassy stretching sides of the bag now expanded to nearly the size of her husband. He made no sound. She knew he was dead, gone, from the stiff strangeness of his face even before the membrane of bag crept up over his features like a sheet drawn in slow motion over the faces of the dead in movies. She felt the breath shuddering in and out of her like sobs.

Light as a cat, something brushed against her ankles.

◆ 34 ◆

Damn Mr. and Mrs. James P. Addison anyway. Brian rang the doorbell with a harder push. He looked out over the streets and waited. Quiet today in the bright sun. All the students not in class were on the beach. He'd heard the surf was good today. Leaves blew about, trash too, the occasional plastic shopping bag puffing with the wind on its uncertain way down the street.

Two seconds more, Brian swore, and the Addisons could go down to the post office for their mail. He'd leave one of those official notices. No way was this package going to fit in the locked postal box they'd set out three years ago. How come they had to be so paranoid, anyhow? Maybe Mrs. James P. Addison ordered jewelry on line. Maybe that was what this package held. He shrugged. Tawdry stuff. Didn't people know that what they got at bargain rates was worth at best the shipping and handling? Catch Mrs. Meg or the Carlquists ordering such shit.

Brian tried one last rap with his knuckles on the door. It unlatched. Oops.

"Anyone home?" Brian said. Loud, so if Mrs. James P. Addison prowled half undressed as usual, he wouldn't get a better view than he was owed. He might slip the parcel on the table at the front door then see if he could lock the door behind him. Yes, the knob had one of those in-handle locks. Easy. But when he stepped in, that one tentative step to reach the table, he stopped. It smelled in here. It reeked, it felt strange. A lot of air movement in the house. He slipped the package onto the table, stepped back. Brian raised his voice and shouted.

"Anybody home?"

No answer.

Call 911? But why, on what justification? He shouldn't have stepped in anyway. He backed out. Stepped onto the safety of the front porch to wait, as if he expected something to happen. But he couldn't stay long.

He left the door ajar, then Brian went around the side of the house. This felt all wrong. The Addisons, with that locked mailbox, leaving the front door open when they were gone? Not likely. The back door stood wide open onto the narrow back path by the pool like the wind had caught it. Brian felt the hair on his nape lift. He looked in.

First thought was that some childish vandal had been at work. Splatters of animal droppings in the house. Duck shit, that's what it looked like. He moved in, listening. Not a sound except the ticking of a pretend Grandfather clock against a wall, electric. He took a few steps down the hall, glanced into the neat white bedroom. No more. Time to call the cops. But no open drawers, none of the kind of disarray he'd have expected from robbers or even kids. He walked back to the living room. Only a huge quantity of duck shit on the nice white linoleum, reflected in all the mirrors.

Something caught his eye. A glint, a sparkle, a piece of jewelry in the brown-and-white pudding of crap on the floor. One heck of a lot of duck doo. There must have been an invasion of ducks, like some scene out of Hitchcock's *The Birds*. He didn't have any desire to touch.

Nine-one-one. His second call to emergency in a month. He leaned down, peering, as a woman answered. What was that rose and white object poking out from the duck shit? Plastic, he guessed.

◆ 35◆

Dwayne did the dishes, efficient and careful. She watched the soapy sponge scrub over the corners of the casserole. He'd told Meg about his dishwashing days.

"And I'm fast," he said, drying his hands on the blue towel. "See?" Anything he put his hand to seemed to get completed incredibly quickly. Except for those shelves in the garage, but she felt sure that would be done as soon as he really put his mind to them.

"Lots more fun to wash up for food I had the luck to eat," he said. "Went hungry a lot in those restaurant dishwasher days."

He insisted she sit and talk while he continued drying. Domestic, comforting in this circle of warm yellow light in the kitchen on a pre-winter night. The dogs settled by the sofa after all chance of food was cleared away. Popeye snored.

"You took care of your dad all those months before he died," he said. "You're a good daughter. Did your brother give you a hand?"

She didn't want to answer.

"No," she said, when Dwayne wouldn't let it pass, standing expectant, his hands not moving to finish the drying.

"He has a career and he's got his own family to worry over."

"How often do you see him? Have Christmas or Thanksgiving together?"

The questions had some quality that Meg didn't understand, an alertness as though the answer mattered more than it should. Dwayne looked down at the mixing bowl in his hands and re-dried the rim before putting it back on the shelf.

"Oh, we haven't seen each other in years."

"Not even for the funeral?"

"He was traveling in Europe on business, I think, when Dad passed, and he told me not to delay for his return before doing the proper things. Considerate."

"Maybe," Dwayne said as if he was thinking something quite different. He bunched up his hands and examined the fingernails.

"So who inherited?" he said.

"Inherited? That's funny you should say that. My brother seemed to think there should be something. But there wasn't. He'd been self-employed most of his life, so Dad didn't even have a pension. No inheritance but the bills for all his medical care that last year. Medicare doesn't cover everything."

"Yeah. So I've heard."

Dwayne shook out his kitchen towel and re-hung it over the oven door before he came back around the counter, his wine glass and the bottle of inexpensive red in his hands. He poured her another half glass then sat down in the adjoining chair, looking comforting, friendly, his brown hair reflecting bits of white in the lamp light.

When Dwayne caught her hand this time, Meg made herself stay still, let him lead, see what he meant by it all. When she had sat down and summed it up, she really did feel that he was courting her, slowly like a gentleman. She knew a lot about him and he'd coaxed nearly every bit of history from her. He tugged her toward him, and she accepted the touch of his lips on her own for an instant before she withdrew, leaned back.

"You don't like?" he said. "I'm sorry."

"I need you to understand, really down deep, Dwayne, that I'll do nothing against the rules of my conscience. Yes, I like you. Lots. Enormously. But I'd never want to lead you on, to expect what I feel would be wrong."

He sat back also, mirroring her.

"Only in marriage?" he said, a mischievous, almost excited note in his voice. His strong face seemed all focused on her, dizzying in its intensity. "A woman like you could make the difference in my life. You're like a gift from God, a light upon the way."

She smiled at him, happiness leaping in her.

"Let's take this relationship one step at a time," she said.

"Oh, I do," he said. "I do. Tell me more about your family. Are you friends with your brother's wife?"

❖ 36 ❖

Past Dogshit Park on the west side by the stands of tall, dark green tules, Nicole saw a duck on the edge of the sidewalk, crouched, too quiet. The duck looked ill, though Nicole claimed no expertise on ducks.

I'm in a hurry. No time for ducks in trouble. Guilt for her own selfishness stopped her. She pivoted on her heel to take another look. Lusterless feathers, sagging head, the eyes looking frightened even in the untranslatable context of bird face. Shit.

She took a step towards it. Female mallard, *Anas platyrynchos*, mottled brown streaky plumage, one of the most common ducks around. Dogshit Park housed a flock that used to sleep on the shores of the pond among the tules. Used to... Nicole shook her head. She hadn't seen a duck around for a while. Nor a crow. Now she thought about it, that was strange. The crows used to spiral up out of Isla Vista like a dancer's shawl in the evenings, cawing to each other. She must be wrong; she'd have to check that. A mistake to theorize in the absence of data, thank you, Sherlock.

Movement caught her attention. She saw a white plastic bag flutter along the curb. God, there was so much trash around, even here in paradise on a clear perfectly sunny day. People were so stupid.... Plastic and paper shed everywhere, in human incontinence. They ought to ban those shopping bags.

Something wrong; a signal missed. Nicole straightened up and stared at the bag. She lifted her hand and felt the light breeze brush the back. The bag moved against the wind. Like Halloween. Nicole took another step. A cross-current down low? Turbulence in the air stream? A single bag couldn't be bad, could it?

Then she saw the sparkle of gemlike brilliance, something catching the sunlight on the bag surface. The bag paused. The glitter intensified—she noted another kind of movement. The sparkly bits moved along the surface of the bag.

What kind of effect was that? While her brain struggled to figure out a logical explanation, she became aware of fear. She had a hard time catching her breath. What was she seeing? Not normal. Cool. Way past cool. Fucking fantastic. Wait until she showed this to Mom and Dad. The bright things were little eyes, or at least that's what they seemed like—they appeared to be congregating to look at her. She stared back.

"Can you hear me?" Nicole said. "Where are you from?"

No, idiot, first things first. She swallowed hard. This wasn't the time to worry someone might see her speaking to a plastic grocery bag.

"I mean you no harm," she said. "Welcome to Earth."

The eyes shone at her. Each maybe ten millimeters across. Cobalt blue centers in white jelly. Maybe twenty of them, which had on first sight been arranged in a band. The translocation of those mobile eyes argued a plastic system, maybe a neural net.

Could something with that kind of amoeba-like ability possibly have intelligence? Maybe not? She felt queasy. How fast was this thing capable of moving? What did it want?

Nicole squatted down, holding her hands open and flat.

"I don't want to scare you," she said. "Can you communicate?"

Had to be an alien. She found herself smiling, thinking friendly at it, anticipation surging up in her, suppressing the unease. How would she persuade it to go home with her? A realization made her spirits soar—she'd been right to think there was something strange about the plastic bags. It wasn't simply a complex about that Dwayne guy and his nasty ways when he'd crept around in the plastic bag costume on Halloween. Boy, she wished Jack were here to see this.

Could she feed it? Make friends in the universal *I'll give you treats if you're nice, too,* way? Supranational diplomacy like the Reese's Pieces in *E.T.*. What might she have in her pockets? She had a bit of gum; that wouldn't do. Ha, a few raisins, woolly from their time in her pocket.

"Do you like raisins?"

It hunched up, the little eyes flowed over to one side as though it wanted to see around her. Wonderful. Then it moved, whipped to the side, past her so fast she heard a squeak force itself out of her lungs.

◆ **37** ◆

Brian felt his head jerk up like someone yanked on his ponytail. He took a split second to recognize the sound—a squeal, not of glee but of suppressed distress. He hurried his steps down the path around the hedge, where he collided into Nicole. Bony elbows and knees, she rebounded off of him then back down the walkway a few staggering steps.

The mail in his hand went flying, the envelopes and flyers scattering about as widely as they possibly could without a wind. But the sound she'd made so worried him that he didn't even look, or think about them. He grasped Nicole's forearm, stopping her. The whites around her eyes showed, he read terror in her blanched face.

"Can I help? What's wrong? Nic?" Maybe his questions came in backwards order, but Brian stood with his feet braced for action, suddenly feeling ten times as alive as he had in months.

"It's there," Nic said, pointing back the way she'd come.

Brian glanced around, sharp for anything, a mugger or a fallen tree, a broken window or a monster.

"What?" he said. "What am I looking for?"

"A plastic bag."

He felt himself scowl, but he wasn't mad yet. Too much fear in her voice.

"What?"

"A plastic bag and a duck," she stammered. He could almost see the effort she made to stop speaking, straighten up and swallow.

"There was a duck, with a plastic bag, one of those white plastic grocery bags you see everywhere, the kind people want to outlaw. The bag jumped past me and caught the duck."

"We can free it," he said, losing her arm and giving it a pat for lack of any better idea of what to do. "Don't get all wigged out."

"No, we can't," she said. "I started over to get the duck loose, but it was like the bag sucked the duck in, swelled up like a jellyfish. I could see through the sides of the bag as it made the duck into pulp—feathers, skin, eyeballs, organs and bones all deliquescing. God, I've been reading too much Lovecraft. The bag turned the duck into goo. Then it looked at me with little bright eyes, all full of duck, pulsing on the ground on the grass by the sidewalk."

"Looked at you," Brian said, thinking maybe he should have kept a hold of Nicole's arm. Drugs. She was on some bad trip. Maybe that new guy she'd been hanging with slipped her something. He'd never thought Nic was the kind to do stupid things. Though you never knew.

"Let me see you back to the house," he said. It would make him late but he could deal with that. Only Puppy would notice.

"It had like a band of tiny eyes… oh, damn it. I'm sorry Brian, I mean Mr.—you know what, I don't know your name properly. I think of you as Postman Brian."

She went down so fast he thought she'd fallen but she scooped up the letters and bills with the stupid flyers, knocking them into order between shaking but deft hands.

"You want to show me this white grocery bag?"

She stood straight with the mail in her hands and looked at him, really looked at him as few people ever look at each other and it made him uncomfortable. But it also gave him the chance to assess her. No dilated or pinpoint pupils, her balance looked good after that swift and graceful collection of the spilled mail. She stood straight. Most people conscious of being under the influence would hide it at all costs, not stand squarely facing anyone who might be able to tell what was wrong.

He'd seen plenty of drugs in his time. Some part of him felt honored in an archaic part of his brain that she would look at him like this as though she really wanted to know what and who he was.

"Let's go," Brian said.

She ran back, Brian jogging after, conscious of how odd it might seem to anyone watching. They could always say they were running to save some trapped animal. What could she have seen? He tried to create all kinds of scenarios, yet when they came near the park, all Brian could recall was the creeping grass he thought he'd seen the first night he met Puppy.

"Did you know I have a dog now? A stray I came across one night. You know a good name for a dog?" he said, trying to get his mind back to a reasonable place, hoping to distract her from this impossible improbable errand.

Nicole slowed, stopped.

"Not right now. It was here," she said.

Grass and sidewalk with a mess of duck shit on it. Brian stepped down into the vacant street to get a longer view, and then he saw it.

The corner of a white plastic bag, semi-inflated, going down the barred mouth of the street drain. Two thoughts hit him as one, that if there was a duck in there, the bag wouldn't have fit between the bars, and two, any duck in that bag was gone. He still stumbled forward, putting his face down, reaching for one fast grab after the disappearing oddly phosphorescent corner.

Brian yanked his hand back, looking in disbelief for the source of pain that seared across his fingertips. Red and oozing blood. Must have missed his grip and scraped the tips, or hit some glass in the drain.

"Nic, was it a *baby* duck?" If so, how much more reason for her to be upset. But it wasn't spring. Not the time for baby ducks. "I'm sorry kid, I think I saw the bag go down the street drain but it's truly gone. No duck rescue today."

"A full-grown female mallard," Nic said with precision. "Your fingers are bleeding."

"Sorry," Brian said. "Guess I just made a fool of myself. There's no way an adult mallard could fit between those bars."

Nicole looked at him, said nothing but he found himself replaying the words she'd spoken. Jelly. Goo. No, he refused the idea.

Brian blew on his grazed fingertips.

"You hurt yourself," Nic said. "I'm sorry—what happened?"

"Like a fool, I tried to snag that corner of a white bag, as if there could be a duck in a drain. Must have scraped them on the concrete."

Nic stared at his hand, her unruly black hair framing her intent face.

"I would say that looks like a chemical burn," she said. "Thank you, though, for trying to come and help. There's nothing here now."

"No, there's not," Brian said, looking around at the apartment buildings, parked cars, with the litter moving slightly where it lay in wind rows on street and sidewalk, some fragments caught in the longer grass. His fingertips ached as if he'd not only cut them but bruised them.

"A name for a dog… Emmett," she said. "You should name your dog Emmett."

"That's a terrible name," Brian said. "I don't want to go around calling a dog Emmett. He'll get a complex."

"Pick a name," Nic said, starting back towards her house. "Any name. Joe, Squid, Thermopylae. What gives a dog a complex is being called 'dog', or 'puppy.'"

How did she know?

"Be careful, Brian," Nicole said. "Watch out."

◆ 38 ◆

"Mom," Nicole swallowed hard again. This had to come out right. "I'd like your undivided attention. We have a problem."

Mom looked up from her book, a startled look on her face, or did it show in the tilt of her glasses?

"Yes?" she said. "Nic, fire away."

"I saw a really disturbing thing today. We have a problem."

"Not sex in the bushes."

Mom had a sympathetic frown now. Proper parental expression in the "I hear you and I feel your pain" sequence, a bit of humor would come next.

"I'm afraid that there's no way to get sex off the streets of Isla Vista," Mom said. "Climate's too kind, and college students will always be horny."

Nicole said nothing. That really caught Mom's attention.

"Okay," she said, "sorry for being frivolous."

"You just wanted to break the tension," Nicole said. "So let me get it out before you comment any more. I think we have some mutation in the local population and it's harmful."

She'd start with mutation; it sounded way more plausible than aliens among us. Nicole saw Mom almost speak and then stop herself.

"I saw something kill a duck right in front of me today," she said. "The attacker looked like a jellyfish, but moved on dry land. About the size of a grocery bag, whitish in color. At first I thought it was a shopping bag, but it went against the wind. It had lots of tiny eyes that shifted about over the surface, so I'm thinking a neural net?"

Mom hadn't interrupted her yet, so that was good. Nicole took a deep breath.

"It stretched over the duck, engulfed it. I could see through the translucent sides, while the duck seemed to melt inside—blood and organs showed then liquefied, too, until it became a slurry. Awful. I ran away, bumped into Postman Brian who went back with me, but we barely saw the bag thing disappearing into a storm drain. Postman Brian tried to hook it back out but all he got was two abraded fingers. He thought the concrete had a jagged edge, but the fingertips look like he burned them. As in a chemical burn."

Mom said nothing. Nicole couldn't tell what she thought from her quiet face behind her thick glasses.

"I think there are more things like that outside," Nicole said. "The crows have gone. You know what the feral cat plus dog population is like—last year there was the guy attacked after dark by a pack of feral dogs. This year you don't even hear them barking by the vernal pools. The ducks are hardly in evidence, though I have to admit there's plenty of duck shit in Freedom Park."

"Remarkable," Mom said. "Why would there be duck shit without ducks?"

"You believe my crazy story?"

"You don't tell it like you're crazy. You exhibit none of the symptoms I associate with schizophrenic delusions, or hysterical fugue. That leaves drug-induced or hypnotic episodes. I'm inclined to put those aside for consideration, but not leap to either conclusion. You saw something you didn't understand, you take no pleasure in telling me. All of that is obvious. What's difficult is knowing what to do. We need data."

Nicole had her hands so tightly grasped together they began to go numb.

"You're kidding."

"Wasn't that supposed to be my line?" Mom took a deep breath. "'*Watch your ass*,' that definitely is my line. I'll watch mine. But I don't see how we can go around warning people until we know more. Getting you or me institutionalized won't help. What do you think is best?"

"Maybe I keep my eyes peeled, and maybe you do, too. I'll talk some more with Postman Brian—he's all over this town on his rounds. He was more shaken than he wanted to show. You know, I always thought aliens would be fun, interesting, educational, and maybe friendly. In spite of Lovecraft."

"Aliens? Is that a parsimonious explanation?"

"I'm thinking it. The bag had eyes that moved in a limited fashion on the surface, so it could study me before it moved them to look at the duck and attack. That argues a fluid organization of tissues."

"I remember a doctor once saying to me that it was a miracle every time you stare into the mirror in the morning that you look approximately the same way you did the night before. Don't think he meant that your eye could move over to the cheek, but he did imply we're a lot more dependent on tissue memory for our appearance than it's quite comfortable to think."

"Ugh," Nicole said. "Mom, I need a hug. Thank you. You can search my room any time you like for drugs. I love you."

Was there any stiffness to that hug, or did Mom truly believe her? How crazy if she did.

❖ 39 ❖

Meg opened her door to the familiar rap. Postman Brian handed her the mail with a smile that came and went fast. She was afraid she'd been rude, but she didn't know how.

"Real mail for a change," he said. She plucked the letter off the top, a business-sized envelope, but her brother's name written in at the top left over his office address. "By the way, did your neighbors, Mr. and Mrs. Addison, say anything to you about going away on vacation?"

"No, they've never really done more than wave at me. Thank you," she said, and nodded. She had oatmeal cookies again and knew the house smelled good, but now she knew better than to offer him any.

He didn't step back immediately as she expected. She thought he looked undecided, worried.

"Have you seen anything strange recently?" he said. "How's Schrand?"

"Getting used to looking like a Manx," she said. "Strange? How do you mean strange?" Meg wondered an instant if he were going to say something about Dwayne living in her garage.

"I don't know," he said, not dismissively, but as though his perplexity went deep. "Nicole was telling me about something killing a duck on the street near the park."

"Nothing like that," she said. She watched his ponytail bob against his blue-gray uniform as he went back down the walk. Meg wished she could have made some kinder gesture, been warmer in her manner, because he looked both puzzled and lonely to her as he walked away. She looked down at her envelope— she hadn't heard from Scott since the usual Christmas card with his scrawl nearly a year ago.

"Dear Meg,

"It's taken me a long time to begin to sort out Dad's effects, especially since you have not given me all the help I expected."

Meg didn't know what he was talking about. What did he need? Her glance skipped to the bottom of the page. His wife had signed the letter, too.

"Our lawyer informs me that the proper course of action will be to first ask you to divulge every detail of your business dealings with our father before his death. We need a full accounting, deposit slips and check stubs, receipts and so on, plus whatever charges you levied against him for his residence in your house.

"It seems strange and unaccountable that his bank savings account contained no more than $3,547. By my understanding and that of my wife, he had at least ten times that amount in his bank accounts alone, but all the information you chose to share indicate only this one account. We need an accounting of all his goods. What has become of the proceeds of selling his house in Sacramento? He owned that property for nearly sixty years and I'm certain…."

An hour later Meg had drafted seven versions of her reply before quitting to clasp her hands. She made a short prayer. It was her fault she'd been too upset to even think about God first, as she should have.

The dogs whined at her. She took them out back to the yard and closed the house door so she could concentrate. She felt like a hunted animal, and what terrified her most was that her brother's voice seemed to come right off the page, every inflection true to life. She couldn't indulge the fantasy that he didn't mean what he wrote nor the potentially comforting idea that someone else, perhaps his wife, had bullied him into writing these cruel, frightening things. She didn't know how to prove she hadn't done the things he alleged. The threat was there. He had plenty of high-powered lawyer friends.

"Dear Scott," she wrote at last. "I don't know where you imagine I could have hidden any money. You should know that, when Dad elected chemotherapy, we didn't know he couldn't be admitted to Hospice while undergoing that type of treatment, so the needs of Dad's last days fell to me, and my bank account covered most of it. If he had other money, I didn't know. If I could have done better negotiating with the oncologists or the nursing assistance program, all I can say is I didn't. Maybe I wasn't smart enough. I have spent the last four years paying off Dad's medical charges, and took your statement at face value when you told me that you couldn't afford to help. I thought you would at least split what remained in his name, but it looks like I can't count on that, either. Now that I have finally finished paying off Dad's remaining debts, you've sent this extremely hurtful letter.

"I don't know what else to say, but I didn't take advantage of Dad, and I didn't steal money from him. If he had as much in savings as you believe, he must have had accounts I never saw, and he received no statements from them at this address. If you can't believe me—"

The doorbell rang and she let the pen drop. She didn't know how to finish that sentence anyway. She got to her feet, blotted her face and eyes on her apron. She hoped she looked presentable, didn't want to shock anyone. She peered past the short curtain on the door panes. Officer Ray? She opened up fast.

"Checking in, Mrs. Meg," he said. "Your neighbors, Mr. and Mrs. Addison, are missing. I'm making the rounds to see if they said anything or did anything to make you think they planned a vacation or went to see relatives?"

"I didn't talk much with them."

"Mrs. Meg, are you all right?" he said, looking sternly at her. "Has anyone hurt you?"

"Oh, only in my mind." She heard the garage door open and shut. She suddenly wanted Officer Ray to be gone before Dwayne came around the corner, though all she said to herself was that she didn't want her day to be any more complicated. There was nothing wrong with her letting Dwayne live in her garage, out of the weather, until he was well.

"I don't know anything to help you. I'm sorry," she said, hoping that would satisfy him.

"What happened?" Officer Ray said, and the direction of his gaze shifted so that she knew Dwayne came in.

"Officer," he said, coming up behind her. "What's the problem?"

"Neighbors missing," Officer Ray said. He glanced down at his computer pad. "Back door wide open, nothing seems to be gone other than identification, front door unlocked, all luggage seems to be there and clothing as well. Mr. Addison hasn't been to work for days, and he wasn't on the calendar for a vacation. Car parked out back. Unlocked. Whole pile of duck crap on the carpet. Coins, loose change with pair of diamond earrings and wedding rings in it." He looked like he thought of something else that he decided not to share.

"Did they owe on bills?" Dwayne said. He smiled, not a nice smile, though Meg could not define why she didn't like it. "Lots of folk just scarper if the bills are more than they can cover."

"I'll note that. Your name is Dwayne, isn't it? Dwayne Wallace?"

"Yes, sir," Dwayne said, and again there was something almost greedy about the way he responded to Officer Ray, as if he were daring the policeman, taunting him. Was it body language or tone? Meg wanted to rein him in, but she saw no way of signaling Dwayne without Officer Ray seeing what she did, which would be too embarrassing.

"I heard something about you on the street," Officer Ray said. "You and Mrs. Fuller having a fight. You remember her, don't you? Tiny little woman with blue eyes and a bad foot."

"Yes," Meg said. "I gave her a ride to the County Health for that foot, but she never showed up for the second appointment. A fight? Between Mrs. Fuller and Dwayne?" her disbelief sounded oddly anxious to her own ears. She couldn't imagine the scene. Dwayne was a gentleman. She'd never seen him do anything selfish or mean.

"Mrs. Fuller said you stole her cans," Officer Ray said, slow and even. "She'd been collecting to pay her bus fare. That's what she told one of our college guys on the Isla Vista foot patrol. Not a professional—he only mentioned it to me the other day."

"Yeah, I remember. We were collecting together, and she didn't want to share at the end, so I took, I dunno, maybe a third of the cans. I spent all day on that job, and I was getting sick myself with the pneumonia that landed me here in Mrs. Meg's kind graces. Maybe it wasn't the right thing. I could have done better. She hit me with some rocks." He grinned and rumpled his hair as if he could still feel the sting of connection.

"So what happened to her?" Officer Ray said.

"Don't know… aw, come on, you're not saying I murdered her and hid the body for two dollars' worth of tin cans?"

"No. She was seen the next day. She didn't have the fare for the bus."

"I'm not responsible. Maybe someone stole the change off her. Could have been. She used to hang out with Charlie, the guy with the dog. We aren't all that we should be, times are hard."

"I can only agree," Officer Ray said. "I'll be on my way." He nodded to Mrs. Meg. "Take care, Mrs. Meg."

It sounded like a warning.

The moment the door closed, Dwayne's smile dropped. "That asshole."

"Dwayne." Meg couldn't take it. Not more contentions, bad language, anger, and betrayal. She wanted a warm arm and a sympathetic shoulder. She felt herself blinking hard to stop the prickle of tears.

Dwayne patted her on the arm, his face softening.

"Don't worry so much, Meg. You carry the weight of the world, but it's not your fault things go wrong. Sorry I sassed."

He went back down the hall into the garage.

◆ **40** ◆

The door opened a few minutes after Nicole's knock. Time enough for Nic to shuffle her feet, look down, and notice that Jack's sneakers bulked twice the size of hers. Time enough for her to realize that she felt far more comfortable on this errand because of Jack's company. The latch clicked, and Meg held the door as though not sure if she wanted to open it all the way. Meg looked upset. Tired around the eyes like she'd cried, and her eyebrows were damp, as though she'd washed her face moments ago. But it wasn't right to confront adults with observations like that. The house felt a little cold, no smells of baking. Only the pleasant colors of autumn in Meg's house seemed as welcoming as ever.

"Hello, Meg? This is my lab partner Jack Kushner. We were wondering…"

"It's been quite a day," Meg said, backing up in invitation. She made that gesture with her hands along the sides of her leaf sprigged apron that Nicole had noticed before, as if she were shaking herself into shape for whatever came next. "Come on in and sit down. I haven't even started anything for dinner. Did you hear that my neighbors, the Addisons, are missing?"

"No," Nicole said. "How, missing?" She accepted an oatmeal cookie off the plate Mrs. Meg offered. Not bad, but Mom's were better. Tasted more brown, somehow.

"Gone. Car in back, unlocked. House unlocked, no goods missing, only piles of duck manure on the floor inside. And some of their jewelry in the duck droppings."

"Now, that is bizarre," Jack said with satisfaction. "That is totally fascinating."

"Spooky, is what," Meg said, but she seemed to be uncoiling from the tension Nicole sensed.

"So the cops are saying, what, that the ducks came in and ate both of them? Hey, weren't they the blond bimbos—sorry, Meg, but really, I don't know if you noticed, but they were like a blond set of Ken and Barbie."

Meg giggled and finally took a cookie for herself, which made Nicole feel much better. She heard one of Meg's renters open and close a door somewhere deep in the house.

"I came by to see how Schrand is doing," Nicole said. "Have you been keeping him inside?"

"Most of the time, and he's recovering physically very well indeed. You gave me the best recommendation for a cat vet."

"Physically?" Jack said.

"He's embarrassed by his tail. It puts his balance off to have only that stubby bit. I feel sorry for him, and he always hides when people come by."

"I'd like to see him, if you're willing." Nicole didn't know how Meg would react to hearing they wanted a sample of the cat after what she'd said about the University and experimentation.

"We were wondering if we could take a little of his fur," Jack said, reaching for a second cookie. "We're doing the high school science project and we wanted to have a bit of cat fur to analyze."

"You mustn't hurt him," Meg said. "The poor cat's been through who knows what...."

"I think taking his vanity down a notch was no loss," another deeper voice said.

Nicole jerked her head up at the familiar tones.

"You," she said.

"Nicole, Jack, this is Dwayne," Meg said as if she disapproved of Nicole's reaction.

"I know you," Nicole said. "You threatened me in the bookstore on Sabado. What is this man doing here, Mrs. Meg?"

She recalled every move and word in that flash of recognition. In defiance of Meg's startled frown, Nicole sat very straight and disapproving. She stared at Dwayne. Postman Brian had mentioned he'd had pneumonia then been housed by Mrs. Meg. She'd sensed Brian didn't like him, and she heartily agreed.

He was as big as she'd remembered, with a way of holding his shoulders that made him look like he was trying to be different from the way he'd been made, passing for someone else. His features verged on heavy, blunt. Broad forehead and slab cheeks, but he was handsome in a way, appealing until you saw the way his eyes spent time assessing, as if to ask what worth you hid from him that he could turn to his own purposes.

"It's you," he said with a little too much humor. "The girl who didn't like to be teased."

"Teasing me is a privilege," Nicole said.

"You have to earn it," Jack said.

Dwayne laughed. Nicole watched him. She didn't want to glance at Meg and see what she made of this.

"You weren't teasing," Nicole said. "You were bullying. It's quite different. You accused me of doing something wrong and said you'd tell on me to Mr. Gorham. Later you acted like you wanted to snatch the book I'd just bought. And why? Why but to play bully?"

"Nicole." Meg lifted her hand in distress, commanding her to stop. "Dwayne is my guest."

"Poor judgment on my part," Dwayne said easily. "I'm sorry I scared you. I'd no idea you didn't understand. That was probably when I was coming down sick; right after that I had pneumonia then ended up in the hospital thanks to good Samaritans. Well, young lady, I do apologize if I offended you by my attempt at humor."

Meg smiled at that. Nicole could tell that she saw nothing wrong in any of this and had no intention of taking any warning about her unsettling renter. Dwayne waved before starting back down the hall.

"I'm going back to work," he said.

"So he's renting…" Nicole said, trying to tame the edge in her voice.

"Not exactly," Meg said, blushing. "He's doing some work and waiting out the coldest time of the year in my garage, so he doesn't have to sleep in his truck. You know, he doesn't have a regular place to live now, and he's looking for a job. If you get pneumonia, it takes a year to heal all the scar tissue."

"Really," Nicole said. She knew it wasn't an adequate response, but she had nothing else to offer.

"About Schrand? May we see him?" Jack said. He leaned forward, his long face intent, as if he cared nothing for the confrontation with Dwayne.

"I don't know," Meg said. She seemed relieved to have a new topic, and Nicole silenced herself. "You won't hurt Schrand?"

"Nope," said Jack. "We just want a bit of fun."

"I'd sound foolish if I refused," Meg said and set her half-eaten cookie down on the table.

Nicole felt something brush past her foot and looked down.

"Hey, puss," she said. She put her hand down and he pushed by, stalking along under the table.

"This is all we need," Nicole said, bringing her hand up, with a few hairs clinging to her fingers; Jack pulled out a snack zip-loc, and they packed up the sample.

"Shy about the short tail then?" Nicole said.

"Yes, he surely is." Meg shook her head. "I'd never have expected him to be quite so jumpy about it, but he is." She picked up the half-eaten cookie and looked it over, her face catching the light so that she looked older and worn.

"I loved your Fiber Arts class." Nicole hadn't planned the words but they seemed to jump out of her mouth, as though feeling sorry about Meg liking Dwayne, and the cat being traumatized had all run together into that *non sequitur*.

"Thanks," Meg said. "It's good to hear that. I loved teaching."

"Would you ever consider going back to teaching? I know the school went under, however much I loved it, but do you think you might offer something maybe to an elementary school that has budget cuts and can't afford to pay for art classes the usual way?"

"There's still a problem of supplies," Meg said. "No, I think not. Besides, I believe the work I'm doing now with the homeless is valuable and serves God."

Nicole felt like she'd stepped way wrong. Time to stop making conversation. It only got her into trouble. When she and Jack headed back to her house with another handful of oatmeal cookies, she watched Jack sideways.

"Stop it," he said. "Stop watching me like you think I'm going to bite you. I'm not a dog."

"Do you believe me?" she said.

"Yes," he said.

"About what?"

"About Dwayne. You always say what you think is true. Even when it's rude. If you're not correct, it's probably an error, or someone is holding your family hostage, *ergo* you'd be lying to save them."

"Oh," Nicole said.

"If you're asking what I think of Dwayne, I think he smells like a psychopath. A bully smart enough to pretend and make nice when he's caught. I wish he wasn't living with her. She seems a little weird but nice. Ditzy. I hope she's not …" He waved his hands.

"She never would," Nicole was shocked. "Never. She's way too religious."

"But she's interested in him, Nic. She wanted to defend him. She wanted to hear the whole story, but she's smart enough to sense that maybe she'd be happier not asking. It's not good."

"She has two renters," Nicole said. "Both women at the local community college, studying nursing and physical therapy or some sort of human-care profession like that."

"Well, I wish one was a shrink because I think Mr. Dwayne should be shrunk down to size."

Nicole had to smile. They passed the bookstore—for once she didn't veer to go in, though Jack looked at her as if to see if she would.

"So you'd believe what I told you?" Nicole said.

"Yes, within the parameters I just gave."

"You even talk like me."

"Appalling."

"So if I told you I saw a plastic shopping bag eat a full grown duck today, you would at least consider the possibility."

Jack nodded.

"And if I described the bag inflating over the duck so that I could kinda see through the sides as the duck puddled down into a soup, you would say what?"

"Do you need new glasses?"

"No, dammit."

"I believe you saw something that made you think that's what you saw. But Nic, I saw an animal eaten by a plastic bag, too. The day before yesterday. It was one of those flea-ridden California ground squirrels, so I think you'd better take my reaction with a healthy dose of skepticism. I'm no more believable than you are."

He stopped in his tracks there on the sidewalk and turned to her, hands stuffed hard into his pockets so that she could see the shapes of his fists.

"I am so relieved that someone else is going crazy," he said. "It gives me hope that this might be a new variant of the flu."

He stared at her, considering. "Does this have anything to do with you getting spooked on Halloween?"

"I wish I knew," Nicole said.

"All the crows have left Isla Vista. They're on the Ellwood side near my house now."

Nicole looked at him, the scowl on his face, the compression of his lips. It took her a moment to realize what he'd said.

"You noticed the crows too."

Jack nodded.

"We had so many, even a month ago." She could envision them, the swirling crowds of noisy roisterers all along the vernal pools, shouldering in heavy rows on the electric lines sagging under their convivial company. Moving through the days, from site to site, sharing the best pickings from nature and man.

"Yup. I heard a scientist from the University complaining that his research had to be adjusted to new sites these past couple weeks because his subject crows moved out of this neighborhood. They're smart birds."

Nicole remembered them making raucous comments, crow tones of criticism.

"They aren't here now, and the guy didn't know why."

"I read a book that said that if there's danger, all it takes is one head crow to warn off a generation," Nicole said.

"So that's us, isn't it?" Jack shrugged. "Two head crows."

"Two-headed crow," Nicole said.

❖ 41 ❖

"Only a kiss," Dwayne said.

The living room felt hot even though the light fell dim and soft on the blue tablecloth and napkins set out upon the table for tomorrow's breakfast. Maybe she'd set the thermostat too high.

Dwayne looked like that movie actor in *Michael Collins*, big, blunt features so appealing, full of a humorous certainty, the smile shy. Coaxing.

"No," Meg said. "It doesn't seem right."

"Your nun-ship's getting in the way," Dwayne said. "Why, do

you feel insecure? I think I might be falling in love and you can't spare a kiss… a kiss on the cheek? A kiss on the forehead? Isn't that safe?"

He bent his head down to look into her face, a slight quirk of amusement still on his mouth.

"I'm sorry I asked," he said. "What does it take to please you?"

"Not much, really. You do please me. But I have to be sure God approves."

"Well, I wish He'd do me the favor of communicating. Maybe a phone call?"

Dwayne cast his gaze up to the ceiling, clasping his hands like a child.

"Come on Lord, do a poor lonely man a favor please? Give us poor souls here a ring?"

She had to laugh, but it felt strange, forced. He was so good looking, so appealing; what was wrong with her?

◆ ◆ ◆

After dinner they shared a second glass of wine, though it was actually Dwayne's fourth, but the glasses hadn't been more than half full, Meg reminded herself. The kitchen held the smells of dinner: spaghetti, tomato sauce, garlic bread, a faint vinegar tang from salad dressing. It sparkled with cleanliness, the golden light of the lamps through fabric shades, cosy.

Dwayne stood behind her as she hung a hand towel.

"But why not?" Dwayne said, re-opening his question. "You know how I feel about you. Won't you give me the least hope that… come on. I know you're not indifferent. Meg, you're so sweet."

How guilty she felt, looking up into his earnest face. He had such a nice mouth now it became tender with feeling. A lock of brown hair fell over his forehead. He turned her away from him then pulled her gently against his chest. His arms crossed over her, close, warm, not too intimate.

"No, it's not that. I can't. I'm upset. There's absolutely too much going on. All I can think about is whether my brother's going to drag me to court."

"Court?"

"I got a second letter. He's alleging I embezzled money from our dad's accounts."

"Second letter?"

"Yes, I'm afraid so."

"You don't trust me," Dwayne said. His body felt still, now wary against her back . "You didn't want to confide what was going on. You don't think I deserve to be told when you're in trouble. I'm not good enough to be allowed in. To support you."

"I didn't want to complain to you. You have your own problems to think about."

"I have problems?"

"Well, you're looking for a job," Meg said.

He made a snorting noise in response.

"And you were living in your truck for a while. I have problems, you have problems."

"Like a nosy landlady who sneaks into my bedroom when I'm gone?"

Meg froze. She felt her whole body changed from the slight resistance where it leaned against Dwayne's secure warmth to a wooden rigidity that he too, must feel.

"Didn't I say I didn't want you intruding in my space?"

She could see their reflection in the dark windowpane, but not enough detail to tell what expression was on his face. Did she need to? Should she straighten? He pulled her back against him. For an instant she felt the gesture held forgiveness, then she realized she was off balance, and he felt like a wall. Concrete hard.

Popeye suddenly nosed up at her, his wet tongue rasping her fingers, muzzle bumping into her closed fingers.

"Let me go," she said, even and steady. She'd dealt with difficult customers before. It was part of her job, she told herself, but Dwayne's arms felt locked around her.

Popeye whined as though he sensed something wrong, but, puzzled in his good dog mind, had no idea what to do. Perry rose from his spot by the counter with a huge dog whuff. She heard his claws clicking on the linoleum. He came to join them, perhaps alerted by Popeye's anxiety. He looked up into her face, his ginger eyebrows lifted as if asking.

"Hey, Meg," a new voice startled them both, Dwayne's arms tightening. "I'm going out for ice cream. Need anything?"

Her roommate, Ming. She hadn't realized Ming was home, nor apparently, had Dwayne. She saw the flash of his smile in the window reflection. He made no attempt to pretend he wasn't embracing her, but his arms loosened. Meg tried to make a face, seeing her grimace in the reflection, but would Ming notice?

"Is Susie home?" Meg said.

"No. She has counseling tonight. See you later," Ming said. She went out the door. With the click of the latch, Dwayne's body moved assertively against her.

"Did you imagine," Dwayne said, and his arms seemed too tight for her to take a full breath, "that I wouldn't notice? That I wouldn't catch the stench of prying? Spying? What kind of shit is that? Who told you to check on me?"

"I don't know what you mean."

She planned how she would put a caressing hand over his right, grasp the thumb, as if she were making peace. *God, let us make peace*; she closed her eyes an instant as if that would wing the intensity of the prayer, but she found her eyes popping wide again, unable to accept lessening her awareness. She had to be alert. Ready. He was a big man.

"I was dying of curiosity," she said, hoping the tremor she felt didn't translate into her voice. Meg tried now for a light note, a slight coquettishness. "I've been wondering about your project for three weeks now, and I simply couldn't stand it anymore. But it looked like you hid everything. Are the shelves you're building hidden in your truck?"

She waited to see if he'd take that. He didn't move, listening as if he wanted more. Popeye pushed his muzzle into her hip now, urgent and uncomfortable, whining again.

"I don't know how you could tell I'd been by. I didn't go past the door. I guess you knew I wouldn't be able to resist. You out-smarted me for sure, but I never thought I'd annoy you by peek-ing in. You must be a real perfectionist, Dwayne. When can I see the shelves?"

His arms loosened, dropped. She felt giddy with relief, catch-ing herself and turning to face him without haste.

"I know women," he said. "Curiosity traps you every time. Like cats."

"Schrand?" she said. Something in his face said he wanted her to pay attention to his emphasis.

"I was so pissed about you invading my room," Dwayne said, looking down at her, lids drooped over his bright eyes.

"Is Schrand all right? You didn't…" She hadn't seen him in a couple of hours. Dwayne wouldn't have hurt her cat, would he?

Shrand meant no harm. He expected the best of people. Dwayne was only teasing, in a cruel way, but still he must be no more than teasing her.

"Don't you trust me?" Dwayne's voice took a lilt on that sickened her. "Trust me with your cats, your dogs, your roommates? Trust me in your house? Doesn't feel like it to me, when you wait for me to be gone and then poke around in my room like you were looking for drugs."

"Schrand?"

"Schrand the bob-tailed cat. What do *you* think I did with him?"

His hand went down to Popeye's head and his big fingers twisted in the dog's ears. One high-pitched prolonged yelp of protest and Popeye whined, as if bewildered that his friend should be so strange, so cruel. It must be a mistake. Popeye stared up at Dwayne, going silent, Perry bristling at his side in matched confusion, and now Meg knew a whole new fear.

"You imagine these dogs will protect you? From anyone?" Dwayne laughed, reaching down, forcing his touch onto Popeye's retreating head. "They're my friends," he said. "Dogs like strength." He stroked down the dog's head hard with a touch that had nothing to do with friendship.

The doorbell jangled. Meg jumped as though struck.

◆ 42 ◆

"Hello?" Mom's tone caught Nicole's attention and she put down her French textbook, which promptly slid off the bed. Nine o'clock, late for a caller.

She had to think about how to keep Mom safe. That was a bad thought. Imagine one of those bags sailing as she'd seen before, over the wall of the back yard. Or whipping around a corner right into Mom's face. She suspected the aliens had some kind of numbing or paralytic ability because the duck had stopped moving immediately. Nicole shivered, remembering the intensity of the duck's yellow bordered eye in the moment before it glazed over and dissolved away with the skull.

Well, who was this? Who would have come to the house?

She came out into the living room. Surprise indeed, it was one of Mrs. Meg's roommates, looking frazzled, though her black hair curved with enviable shining smoothness about her face. Her voice sounded low and anxious, urgent.

"I'm Ming Chen. One of Meg Burdigal's roommates. I don't know if you remember....I'm scared for her," the young woman said. "I think he's angry, that homeless guy, she invited to stay, Dwayne. cagey character. I'm afraid of him. He's given me the creeps for weeks."

"Did they see you leave?" Mom took her jacket off the hook by the door and slid her arms in that curious smooth action that Mom had when she was in a hurry. Last time was when Nicole needed stitches in her arm from catching it on the fence by the back of Gordon's Market.

Nicole pulled on her own coat, shivering into it against the draft from the front door. Well, at least if Mom went out, she'd be there too, with her eyes peeled for wafting shopping bags. She sounded like a nut even to herself. It made her miss Jack.

Mom looked at her for a second's hesitation, her eyes black and narrowed in consideration.

"Yes, we can use you," she said. "Is Jack around?"

"I'll text him. What's up?"

Until the words came out of her mouth, Nicole hadn't realized how much she took for granted—that Jack wouldn't mind the interruption and that he'd be ready to help.

"It's the homeless man Meg invited into her house. Ming here says she heard them having a disagreement, and some tone in it triggered her to get help from us."

"I'm taking a domestic violence class," Ming said. "There are signals. His asking Meg 'you're not afraid of me, are you?' was a biggie." She seemed too nervous to want to say more. They went out the door, Nic checking it latched properly, then hurrying along the street after Ming and Mom. Nic cast a wary glance about but it was hard to see if there might be any unnatural garbage around.

Nicole texted one more burst to Jack. "Be careful. Watch for bags."

"Let's all go in together—keep looking casual," Mom said, but when the three of them heard a dog cry out in pain, Mom got up the last steps to the door as if she flew, and leaned on the doorbell. Ming opened the door for her.

"Sorry about that—I forgot I didn't need to ring. Hello, Meg, and this is Dwayne? I don't think we've met."

He stood there like a man in the sulks, but recovering with every instant, straightening his shoulders, bringing a smile to his face, though Nicole caught a sidelong glance at Ming that made a prickle run up and down her spine. Dwayne watched Nic and his face changed again, as if he knew he'd lost the chance to grace his way through this.

Mom sat down without invitation, and Nicole noted how different her body language had become. Cover Mom's plain round face, and you would never know who this person was. She projected a sense of maleness. Confidence bordering on arrogance, and Nicole remembered Dad joking, "If you think I'm Alpha, hey, you should see your mother when she decides to unmask." Sitting was a calming signal—Nicole had read enough about mammalian communication to know that. Sitting first gave the message that Mom didn't feel any threat from Dwayne—the gesture dismissed him. But wouldn't it make him angrier?

"Who are you people?" Dwayne said, a flush intensifying in his face. "What are you doing, coming in without invitation? I know Meg didn't have plans for you all to be here. What kind of intrusion is this? A *surprise* party?"

He looked at Meg, gave an elaborate shrug, seemed to force his shoulders down and smiled. Charming, now, tilting his head to one side. Could he change the playing field? Mom looked at Meg, waiting.

"So did Missy Ming freak out because I'm here? Ming never approved of Meg inviting me in, me being homeless and sick and all that. Down on my luck. Maybe she worried I was contagious."

Nicole felt fierce satisfaction to see him off his stride. She could see him changing his approach, trying for sympathy, getting no resonance from this audience. She spared some attention for Meg. Now, if Meg bought that line of malarkey, they would have to retreat… or would Mom have another tack? Meg's face looked sick, washed pale and her eyes seemed those of a woman who hasn't had a good night's sleep in weeks. Nicole suspected it was simply the way that Meg's particular coloring and temperament responded. Meg was the sort to think any problem was her own fault first.

Mom said nothing, waiting.

"Come on," Dwayne said. He took up his half-filled glass from the table and pulled out a chair.

"I can appreciate you worrying for Meg. It's a great thing for her to have friends like this. But what do you know about Meg and me? I haven't seen you around, except for Ming, who never had any time for Meg these last few weeks since I moved in. What is your business here? C'mon Meg, do you really feel like you need interference?"

"Look at the dogs," Nicole said.

Both stood, restless, unsettled, no wagging. They hadn't barked at the influx of new people. Nicole had never seen them so quiet, so dismayed.

"I heard a dog in pain," Mom said. "Did Popeye get hurt?"

Meg had both arms at her sides. Nicole couldn't see if her fingers were relaxed or tight. Without saying anything, Meg looked away from them all, and Nicole could see her chest rise and fall as though she took a deep breath or a sob.

"Do you think I'd hurt you?" Dwayne sounded caressing, his deep voice full of confidence.

"Tonight's the night you move out," Meg said, turning her head to look at him.

Dwayne surged out of his seat. Meg flinched, but Mom didn't move a muscle. The front door swung open, and Jack erupted in, short of breath as if he'd been running.

"You fucking bitches, and your Jack dog, too," Dwayne said. "The sooner I'm out, the better for me. The worse for you."

He lurched to his feet and went, his shoes noisy in the hall. They listened to his banging door then sounds of furious activity.

Meg turned, her lips white. "I feel just awful," she said. "I can't talk."

Jack stepped forward and pulled out a kitchen chair for her. She sat down like one exhausted. Nic wanted to shake her, make her take action, any action. Please Meg, do something.

"Thank you," Mom said. "You had a choice to throw us out instead, and you didn't."

"No, he was scaring me. All of a sudden. We went from a good friendly relationship to something turned inside out. I could taste it. I didn't want it to go so wrong, you know?"

"Yes," Mom said.

"Do you think he'll break the stuff in his room?" Jack said, cocking his head to listen to the sounds coming from down the corridor.

"I don't care," Meg said. "I just want him gone. It's so sad."

Ming sat down on the couch and pulled her feet up under her, hugging her knees.

"Mrs. Meg," she said. "I'm still afraid. What if he comes back later?"

A faint mew came from behind the couch, then Schrand bolted from under it to the kitchen.

"We'll see Dwayne Wallace gone, and then both of you and Susie can come home with us," Mom said. "I think a slumber party is exactly what's called for. I have a movie, *The Sixth Sense,* and if that doesn't get your mind off of this evening, nothing will. Scare the crap out of you. Popcorn and nuts. Ming, why don't you pack an overnight bag and Meg, you too. Ming, if you could text Susie to let her know she should come home as soon as she can and get her own stuff together, that will help. We don't need to let Dwayne know he's shaken you at all. We'll get your locks changed tomorrow. It'll be OK."

"Mom?" Nicole pulled Mom aside as soon as Ming and Meg disappeared to their rooms. "Can I run down the street? I'll take Jack. I think I have an idea who could house sit. Meg won't want to leave the place empty."

Nicole held the door open for Jack. Popcorn. A comforting memory, homey. That was what had made her think of Brian. Nicole wondered if the nature of memory was to soften, to reassure because you always knew how everything came out in the end of a past event. Maybe the opposite for people who had all bad memories, like Postman Brian. She'd been wondering about him. He always seemed to slide back down into some place cold and unfriendly. Maybe he needed friends. Maybe he needed Prozac. Maybe she needed to stop thinking. She realized that under stress her brain went on fast forward, nattering, filling the empty spaces.

❖ 43 ❖

Brian had set the empty bowl from his soup in the sink, when someone knocked, a hesitant knock that became bolder as it hit the third repeat. The brown dog exploded into purposeful barking.

Brian looked about his bleak kitchen, amazed, breaking from his automatic motions, the mechanical acceptance of where and how he was, suddenly annoyed at the flickering florescent light bulb he'd meant to replace months ago. What a dingy place. Had anyone come to visit in the past five years except for a brown dog?

"Quiet, Emmett," he said. The dog paused as though wondering whether he really meant it.

In the ten steps to the door, with Emmett dancing around his feet, he flashed through possibilities. It was someone who'd made a mistake in the address. It was Josie come to ask him to take her back. It was someone looking for Emmett, someone who had a claim.

At the last thought, he stopped with his hand on the doorknob glancing down at the small animal standing rigid with attention by his ankle. No, surely not. Emmett had been too ugly, too neglected, too full of worms. He didn't resemble any known breed, having aspects of an Affenpinscher, a border terrier, plus some pug. Hadn't even been neutered until Brian took him to the vet. Brian raised his hand, pointed at Emmett, and Emmett sat.

Brian opened the door.

"Yes?" he said. At least he recognized the two standing there. Nicole with her tall friend, the guy she'd had around with her over the last few weeks. Jack.

"Sorry to interrupt," Nicole said when he ushered them in. Emmett sat as though glued but his nose wobbled with excitement while his curly tail smote the linoleum.

"I know it's a presumption, but I was hoping you might be able to help us."

"Sit down, then you can explain," Brian said. "Do you want a Coke or something?"

"No, thanks, I didn't mean—"

"I'm Jack Kushner. I go to school with Nicole. May I have a Coke?"

Nicole gave him a look that made Brian smile. He hoped he had a Coke somewhere in the fridge. He didn't suppose rum would be appropriate. He released Emmett to run with a flick of his fingers. Damn, that dog was smart.

"I named him Emmet," Brian said. He felt silly saying it.

"Emmett," Nicole said. The dog trotted round her, his ugly face grinning up, pink tongue sticking out.

"I told you that name would give him a complex," Brian said.

Thank God there was a Coke in the fridge. He came back, set it down. Josie would have given him hell for not pouring it into a glass, but he figured he didn't have to answer to her any more. All his glasses were spotty anyway.

"Thanks. Emmett? Isn't that a weird name for a dog?" Jack said.

"Sure as hell," Brian said. "It's Nicole's fault. She named him. Gave the dog a complex. I can tell."

Nicole didn't take the bait.

"You're looking prime, Emmett," she said. "Brian, I hope you don't mind my calling you that. We just came from Meg's where—"

"Where Nicole's Darth Mom, not to be confused with Darth Maul who is a pussycat by contrast, just evicted Dwayne from the premises. He's packing."

Surprised, Brian felt himself smile.

"What? I thought he and Mrs. Meg...?"

"Close, but escaped by a whisker," Nicole said. "You know how straight-laced she is. The lacing may have saved her from something a lot worse or at least a lot more complicated."

"He's a bad actor," Jack said.

"And Meg?"

"She said the words of dismissal, with our back-up."

"*Darth Mom*, I like," Nicole said. "We're moving Meg and Ming and Susie all to our house for the night, but we're a little worried about Meg's place. Can't change the locks until morning."

"I can come," Brian said. "I'll move in with Emmett for a day or two so long as her dogs can deal with that."

"Nice, Brian, you just got major points from me—you didn't even make me ask. I think she would have brought the dogs to us rather than leave them alone, but if you're willing..." Nicole said. "Do you think Dwayne might hurt them if he's still hanging around? Will you be OK?"

He noticed Jack finishing off the Coke as if he'd done a liquid version of a sword swallow.

"Not to worry," Brian said. "I'll be there. Nic, what about your problem with the trash? All fixed?"

He didn't want to embarrass her, but Jack was the one who answered.

"No code needed, I've seen the plastic bags too. It's not over. Watch out, Brian. They're out on the streets and on the beaches. I'm trying to find out how many pets are gone. Animal Control records. Brian, what about those neighbors? The young couple?"

"The missing neighbors. Only thing left in the house, I hear, was piles of duck crap and in them a couple of pieces of jewelry and a watch, and some odd bits of silvery metal. And a finger."

He hadn't meant to admit that last. Shit.

"A finger," Jack said.

"Yes, a finger."

"And you didn't think this was worth mentioning to everyone on this street; why?"

"Good one," Brian said, but the back of his neck prickled again. "Maybe because I'd feel stupid and I'm still not convinced the story's real? You must have watched *The Blob* on the Sci Fi channel. Now there are two of you running this gig."

"Show Jack your fingers," Nicole said, and there wasn't any suggestion of humor in her expression.

He couldn't refuse without looking silly, so he shrugged and put out his right hand.

"Nice," Jack said, pulling out a hand lens from his shirt pocket to examine the rasped tips. "I agree. Chemical burn, base or acid, but it looks like a localized necrosis, so my guess is a base."

"Shit, kids," Brian said. "I grazed my fingers on the culvert surround. Next thing I know you'll be saying I have zombie tooth marks on my scalp."

"Did I see you using a metal detector once in the park?" Nicole said. "Could I borrow it?"

"Nope, it wasn't mine," Brian said. "Borrowed it from one of the homeless, Old Cricket, after I lost my favorite jackknife. Sorry. But he's around so you can ask him. I recall him saying he made a fair amount in spare change off that thing."

"Why a metal detector? What are you planning, Nic?" Jack said.

"Fillings, pieces from glasses, rings, zippers, pocket knives. I'm hypothesizing these things don't engulf metal. I think we need to find evidence of murder."

◆ **44** ◆

Meg slept so hard that to say she fell asleep felt like the literal truth to her when she woke in the guest bedroom at the Carlquists' next morning. A note on the counter told her to do as she pleased for breakfast, but she was already going to be late to the church. She'd forgotten to bring a hairbrush. She borrowed Nicole's before tying her graying shock in a business-like pony tail. Was that some message to herself and her hopes? Was pulled-back and business-like the best she would ever do?

When she came in sight of St. Athos's church, she could tell that no one else had opened up the Havens yet. A ragged line of folk of all sorts, adults, children, couples and stragglers, turned to watch her approach.

"So Jennifer isn't here?" she asked Ginny, who was nearest the back door by the trailer. She could see her breath on the morning air. Surprisingly cold for this early in November.

"No one is," Ginny said. She cupped her hands before her face to blow into them. "You're late."

"I'm sorry," Meg said.

She started coffee and hot water, got out all the supplies that she'd readied last night, noticed that the entire main building felt cold. Two nights in the low fifties already—she'd seen in the paper they recorded fifty-four Fahrenheit for the night low a couple of days ago. This promised to be a bad winter.

She'd have to deal with the county or school district to see if they might provide temporary shelter when the rains came and night temperatures fell. Fifty-degree nights touched low enough to kill those without a roof. The diaper factory cafeteria stood closer and had way fewer forms to fill out. She'd need God's own grace to help her deal with any of those administrators better than she'd dealt with that pharmacist. When things slowed down at the breakfast service, she'd take a moment for prayer. For now, God would have to take her promise to get back to him. As if He waited on a phone line, in order of calls received.

"Mrs. Meg?"

She looked up. It was Dolores, so aptly named a woman of sorrows, her swollen face and eyes habitually brimming with tears. If you looked down at her feet shaped like blocks, wrapped in scarves and old towels, they told the rest of the story.

"Weren't no shoes made to fit feet like these," Dolores would say, and laugh. Hard to believe she wasn't much over fifty. Edema, nothing to be done but the bed rest she couldn't find, the new kidneys she couldn't qualify to get. A no-salt diet was a fantasy for street folk. Dolores needed dialysis, but her authorization hung up in the system. Meg made a note to herself—call again, rant and rave that they'd have a death on their hands if that authorization didn't clear.

"Good morning, Dolores."

"Can I talk with you? Only a minute, please, Meg Ma'am?"

"Sure," she said. "Just let me feed folk first if that's OK?"

Dolores nodded.

Meg hurried getting the job done, answering friendly greetings, requests, and demands, then finally went to sit with Dolores on the bench under the pepper tree.

"Don't think I'm going to make it," Dolores said. "Don't know if I want to. This misery," she shook her head. "You tried real hard, Mrs. Meg, and I want you to know I appreciate it. But I'll look to heaven, I guess. I miss my babies so."

Four pregnancies. She'd smoked and drunk and drugged through all of them, and foster care swallowed every child. Meg patted Dolores' hand, unable today to think of anything good to say. She'd run dry.

"But I heard good news, Mrs. Meg, if you'll tell me it's really true."

"Yes, Dolores?"

"You kicked Dwayne out of your place?"

Her question hit Meg in a new way. What had she been doing, picking one man to put in her house? What had her motives been? Initially, had she been right to shelter Dwayne at all when there were so many others, so many like Dolores? What would such help have meant to this woman, with her constant pain? What about the newcomer, Johnny, who really needed a psych admit but wasn't going to get one because he threatened no one but himself?

She nodded, and Dolores's face squeezed up in pleasure.

"We're so glad," she said. "He was a mean one, but how could we say it and make you feel like we were all against you having a bit of fun with a good-looking man in your bed? Like we was all jealous? You would've thought bad of us. We know. Maybe he'd get better, Ginny said. I said no man at all is better than a bad one, but we couldn't come tell you, so thank the good Lord. We are going to be happy today, Mrs. Meg. Thank you."

Meg swallowed hard. She wanted to cry, but she couldn't let Dolores see.

"Thank you, Dolores," she said, and patted the swollen hand, trying to smile, but she settled for a nod as the best she could do. She must numb herself down until she could get someplace private. But not now, not now when she had work to do and people who counted on her. It was only some hours later that she realized she hadn't disabused Dolores of the idea that she'd been sleeping with Dwayne.

Lord, she thought, is that part of the humiliation I earned, that you let me see so much so late? My heart is raw about him, for my wrongful hope, but what did I dream that was not true? Where does Dwayne belong and where do I?

She sat at her rickety desk in the trailer and looked at her folded hands. Was Karen's objection a lack of charity as she'd thought at the time? Or had it been a message? Was there a way she could turn her garage into temporary housing for the very ill who couldn't stay in the hospital when they needed it, yet couldn't, for various reasons, go to the other shelters in town? She had to rent two rooms to pay her mortgage plus taxes. What renters would put up with a vagrant population living in the garage? Ming and Susie had been remarkable in their acceptance, now she owed Ming deep thanks for her interference last night.

"Lord," she said. "Help me to know what to do."

She reached for the telephone. Time to call again, push harder, and get Dolores's case moved on.

◆ ◆ ◆

"Look, Mrs. Lewis, I'd like to speak with your manager, Mrs. Patty Histler, if I may. We're looking for permission to use the factory cafeteria tonight for sheltering. Oh, she stepped out? Could you ask her to call me, or if convenient, she could drop by. I'm here at the office for St. Athos Outreach until five today."

So many times, people from the papers or the TV station, even the radio, asked Meg why on earth more of these homeless weren't in the regular shelters, the year-round places that gave a person a room with a closet, a shared bath, even some food. If you were poor, they said, you should admit it, not go out littering the streets, embarrassing the public by sleeping on benches.

Meg looked down at the bills on her desk. Who would think

that those massive boxes of vanilla wafers cost so much? She could already feel the chill growing as the day wore on. She should have brought a warmer jacket.

It's complicated, Meg remembered saying to an interviewer. We have folk who are sure the government is trying to imprison them, folk who have the kind of demons in their heads that won't let them fit in a year-round shelter. Some are yellers, or violent when the troubles are on them; they see things that aren't there. Since the general push not to spend money on "unnecessary incarceration" some years ago, a flood of borderline patients ended up on the streets.

Families who at first said they'd oversee or house a relative changed their minds when they found out how hard it can be to offer endless patience and monitoring, much less loving care. It was hard enough to get the kids to school in the morning, hard enough to keep the house in order, hard enough to try and teach the kids good manners at the table without adding Uncle Mark shoveling food with both hands, or spitting it out saying it was poisoned, giving everyone the evil eye.

It was way too hard if the impaired uncle took to shouting or bellowing so the neighbors complained. Then one day you'd find the sticky little pile of spat-out pills hidden in the couch and realize that watching Uncle swallow a sip of water after inserting the pill into his mouth, didn't mean he'd taken his medication. Next thing a person knew, husband would come home to say his second job had been cut back to even fewer hours. It was too short a leash and too long a year.

She remembered Winsome finding that human leg and shuddered. Who knew what terrible event that signified? What about Winsome's disappearance? She knew Officer Ray thought serial murder now, but he needed a method. Heck, he needed a clue. He needed bodies. Maybe each was an individual, single tragedy? A man sent off by his own family died in the bushes and maybe the feral dogs...?

Then think about those fake homeless guys whose guts she'd take for shoestring, two who owned fancy houses, one had two, one in Miami and the other here in Santa Barbara. Both those rich guys did the homeless act like it was an "extreme adventure." They took from this table Meg put food on. They were first at the warming shelters, claiming the best blankets. They panhandled and cussed the cops, then, when the weather really went to hell, they took a taxi or a jet headed back home for the Jacuzzi.

Don't get her started on the business of medications, alcohol and cigarettes. Anyone in a regular shelter has to hand their contraband over or get rid of it before they check into a regular shelter. What's the harm in an old man drinking his can of beer? Well, the rules say he can't stay under the roof if he drinks it, so if he wants that comfort, he's going to have to make do outside. One beer equals no cot.

Cigarettes give a lift, warmth, plus they kill appetite, really handy when you have no food. Meg hated smoking, but she saw the attraction.

As for drugs, most doctors don't give chronic sufferers enough help with pain. Everyone jumps at the name of an opium derivative, but sometimes it's the only thing that blunts pain. Not only for bone cancer patients, but for a long list of problems—argh, it did no good to think the same old thoughts that got her angry all over again…. Meg paged through the work on her desk without even seeing it, dreading the fact that she had to talk to Patty Histler, the woman who managed the diaper cover factory building. She could see the blond-dyed woman's plump foundation-coated cheeks puffing with exasperation. No, I'm not giving today. Meg looked up as Patty Histler walked in. Think of the devil.

"The Health Department posted a hazardous weather alert for unsheltered homeless people for tonight. May we use your cafeteria again for a warming shelter?" Meg made her voice gentle and positive. The high school gym had a play being performed; she'd been advised it would be too hard to coordinate that location.

Patti's face folded into a no.

"Not me. You don't come to me anymore. I came by to see what progress you made on my complaint about the trash left when we last permitted your people to sleep in the cafeteria."

"I can only assure you that I checked the space myself before we left at seven-thirty that morning. At that time, we had the cafeteria in as clean a condition as when we arrived—in fact, we'd done a patrol of the outdoor sitting area as well, and the picnic area. I must have missed something. I do sincerely apologize."

"It was a mess. I heard that announcement about the weather, and I wanted to get to you as soon as possible to make it clear we will no longer support your vagrants by giving them free housing. It's not even going to be that cold. This fall has been one of the warmest on record."

"The Health Department has officially notified—"

"You can't know it's going to be that cold. Besides, that last time one of the employees said the south corner smelled like someone did his business there. On the floor." Patty's lipstick nearly matched the cherry pink of her woolly sweater, but missed by a few degrees toward orange.

"I can assure you—"

"Of what? That they only left fleas? Just because your church has decided it has a holy cause, I'm not obligated."

Meg found herself thinking about Ilene's sleeping bag. She'd tried washing it, and now it was more like a bag of dead rats than a sleeping bag. Some days Meg wished she could go buy about fifty sleeping bags from all the thrift stores in town and pass them out.

"They really need our help, Patty."

"Like hell. I see them in line in front of me at the grocery with their food stamps."

"A lot don't receive food stamps."

Richard, for one, who feared that the tax men were after him, and so didn't dare sleep in an all-year shelter or sign up for food stamps. He knew they planned to wash his brain, he said, and put nails in it.

"They need to learn how to work, that's what'll help them. I don't want those filthy bums on my clean floor again."

Patty turned, walked away, with Meg chasing after her.

"They're human beings, Patty." She knew that both George and Charlie could hear her, but her voice escalated up anyhow. "Like you and me."

"They aren't going to freeze," Patty said. "It's not freezing."

"No," Meg said against that obdurate broad back in its cheerful cherry sweater. "It doesn't have to freeze to kill. People sleeping out of doors start dying around 50 degrees if they don't have good clothing. If it's raining...."

But Patty didn't stop.

Meg made herself head over to the church office. She was in luck. There sat Father Stephens at his desk writing, his elegant fingers balancing his stubby pencil as though it were a wand. She rapped on the doorframe, looked down at his balding head, feeling guilty.

"You want me to call?" Father Stephens said.

"How did you guess?"

"I saw Patty heading out of your office looking like she'd won the lottery," Father Stephens smiled, but he looked so tired. How much trouble they all caused him. "I'll call her supervisor, Mr. Robeson," he said.

◆ 45 ◆

Home early, Nicole finished her French then turned with relief to Biology. She could read through the chapter, do the exercises in no time. Jack might show up for cookies. She'd refrained from having any yet.

She planned to walk down to the university to escort Mom from her laboratory on campus. Jack's company would be a comfort, also an extra pair of eyes. They hadn't talked much about the plastic things, but neither of them had seen anything for several drizzly days. She kicked herself for the urge to forget, to dismiss the inconvenient and unsettling memories. Funny weather, as though the clouds couldn't quite decide if the rainy season would start yet. Surfers still went out, paradise still in place.

She had to sharpen up. Did Jack dare talk with his parents about the bags? Did he worry about them? The crows hung out these days in the eucalyptus grove near his house, so presumably his neighborhood was safe. There had to be something about Dogshit Park. Incidents all seemed to center there.

She startled to hear the front door. Hah, it was Mom. Early tonight, with the sunlight still strong. Mom in a rush, from the sound of it. Nicole went to her bedroom doorway to say hi.

"Nic," Mom said, straight and precise. "It's not really bad news, but we have to change plans. There's been an accident. Your Dad got bumped by a car in DC at one of those stupid crossings, probably talking too much to see a car run the light. They say it's a cracked tibia, maybe a dislocated shoulder, but they also found a heart arrhythmia on admission that they want to check. So, I'm on the seven twenty to LAX, and DC by morning."

Nicole nodded. No time to freak.

"How can I help?" she said. She experienced a perverse relief. This would get Mom out of the danger zone, give some time to sort this plastic alien thing out. She hated the idea of her father suffering, but she knew she was expected to keep her head.

"What shall I do with you?" Mom said. "I know you've been worried about safety, and I hate to leave you here alone."

Mom took clothing from her closet, deftly setting items neatly folded, one after another in her suitcase. Formal clothes. Tailored jacket, oxford shirts, silk scarves. Mom was going loaded for bear. She might sound reassuring, but she was going with the professional look to deal with unknown doctors.

"Nice, Mom. You know what, we'll sit tight here, Meg, her renters, and me."

"Call her, please," Mom said. "With all the strange stuff, it might be a good idea to make sure she can stay here with you. Otherwise you know I'd trust you alone, but this isn't about trust."

Nicole took a deep breath. She picked up the notepad with Meg's cell number. Dialed, got Meg on the third ring and explained fast.

"I'd love to," Meg said, sounding as though offered a treat. "But there's a bit of a complication. Hope your mother doesn't mind. I'd need to have you hang out with me at the homeless shelter tonight–I think we'll be in that factory where they make rubber diaper covers, over by the church. We're having a cold night with possible rain, and I'll have to be at the shelter admitting folk until ten o'clock. Then we'll head for your place. She won't mind that, will she?"

It sounded interesting, if only the bags weren't out. But now wasn't the time to harp about that to Mom.

"Don't worry," Nicole said. "I'll tell her, then call you back."

◆ ◆ ◆

"OK, Nic," Meg said. "Here's the count for our shelter tonight. Four women, two kids on this side. All quiet. On the men's side, thirteen trying to sleep, one a bit drunk, but his friend Eric trying to keep him down, so we won't throw them out. We've got a dry shelter here in more than one definition. My coworker, Joe, wanted lights out, but I want to see what's happening. We lock doors at ten. Lincoln will take over around eleven for me, and we can go home."

"I have to get up out of my bag and shut you; there's going to be some shit going down over there."

Nicole jumped. Sounded like a radio suddenly given juice with the knob turned on maximum. Who was talking over there? The drunk guy?

"Kick you in the gut if you don't shut the fuck up, man. I'll kick your frigging head in. Need my goddamn sleep. Didn't fucking come here to listen to no fucking opera all the goddamn night."

"Can't do that, friend. Lie down and let him be," a deep growly voice somewhere near the eruption, slow and certain. Nicole thought it might be the man Meg had introduced as Eric early that evening.

Nicole saw Meg lift her head, her face peaceful but alert in the strange glow of her laptop screen. Writing something, whether letters or maybe requisitions for her job.

"He gives me bad dreams," a new voice sounding close to tears. "I can't deal. He's gotta shut up."

"We're all here to keep warm, friend. Lie down, cover up your ears, enjoy the warmth. Sleep's gonna come. You'll be OK," the Eric voice said.

The first man's voice died down into muttering. Nicole hoped it was over. Her stomach had turned at the sudden emotion in this surreal room of huddled bodies, stale sweat gone rancid with a strange sweetish odor over all. 9:40 p.m.; most guests already sleeping, or faking it.

"Don't make me get up." It was Eric again, as if the contagion of irritation grading into anger had gone from the first man into him, to grow there.

"I don't want no trouble. Don't want no noise."

The snoring man turned, his breath bubbled into a sleeping moan like a sick man. Maybe he had something. Bronchitis, pneumonia. Nicole didn't want to get ill.

"Quiet hours start at eleven," Meg said, her voice pitched low to carry across the various people with their heaps of belongings. She sat on the women's side of the cafeteria. Nicole, who'd drifted over towards the serving counter, walked back.

If Lincoln made it in time, Meg and she could walk home. Nicole didn't know how she felt about that; to go back into the open again with poor visibility seemed dangerous. Yet this place with these people made her uncomfortable in so many ways that she couldn't even hope to count them. The list started off with guilt, because she had a home to go to. Because she passed the homeless every day without a smile, or a quarter out of her slim allowance and vanishing summer job earnings. Then there was the smell—every time her skin prickled the least bit, Nicole found herself looking to check, some part of her mind certain that she'd picked something up—a flea, lice, or an unnamed disease.

She'd noticed how many of the men and women who came in looked like they wore every bit of clothing in their possession whether for warmth or to keep their goods from thievery, Nicole couldn't guess. Skins bronzed not with a simple day's worth of sweat, but with weeks of outdoor burnish. Some wore clothes so stiff-sleeked with dirt, skin oils, perspiration, that the fabric had an odd gloss, a smell like rancid butter, excrement and vomit. What did you do for toilet paper when you were homeless? She thought she recalled some folk carrying rolls among their goods.

Maybe primitive man smelled like this, before parts of civilization fell in love with hot water, soap and flush toilets. As if on cue, a thin man by Meg's desk bent close to her. Nicole admired Meg then, who looked at him as one looks at any man, a slight smile of interest, without a back lean to her body, though he looked too close for comfort. One of those who didn't know what the approachable radius should be. He was black, spidery tall like a daddy long-legs.

"I got a shower this morning. The water kind of leaked all over me, and it was mucho frio, Mrs. Meg, but I washed. I really washed. With a bit of soap, genuine Ivory, that I found at the laundromat. My first shower in three weeks, Mrs. Meg, but that sure is one good thing. Ain't it just."

"Yes," Mrs. Meg said. "It sure is, Tony."

As if one shower in three weeks could get a man clean. Nicole bet the dirt ground deep in, right down into the pores as unwashed day followed day. You'd have to steam clean, sauna maybe, then hit the showers three, four times to get a man like that clean. Meg smiled, nodding as though she could imagine exactly what he meant, and agreed how good it felt.

How many people here now? A dozen men, one sitting up with his back to a pillar, what was he doing? Rolling a joint? A cigarette?

"Hey, man, you can't do that here," someone among the long, prone shapes said.

"Who's making noise over there?"

"There's no smoking indoors."

"But I'm rolling my own."

"No smoking anything, kid, in here. Lookit the sign."

"What good is it? I get comfortable, get my feet to feeling again, and now I can't have my smoke?"

"Go out."

"Shut the fuck up," Eric, snarling again, his stable friendliness all gone. Worn off.

"Go outdoors."

"Don't want to. Need to keep my feet warm."

"Besides, another fifteen minutes, they'll close the doors. Save it for morning. You don't wanna go out and have them close all your stuff in here, and you outside."

"Do I have to come over there?" This sounded like a real threat. "A man needs his sleep."

"What good is it, can't have my smoke?"

"You make one more whine, and you'll eat that fag."

"Let him go. Bag'll get him, that's for sure, and good riddance."

Nicole stopped in her pacing along the divide of the room. Who said that?

"Bag?" she said, and her own voice sounded so strange to her, so alien to her now that she wanted to stuff it back down her throat.

"Shut the fuck up." Eric sat up.

Meg's night assistant, Joe, went over, made some low-pitched conversation with the man who'd been rolling his own and Eric. After he'd gone, Nicole started over there, her legs shaking.

"Eric," she said, soft, some instinct knowing she had to approach him first. "It's Nicole. My name is Nicole."

You give a man your name and you give him power. If you call him by his name and don't give him yours, you put him in your power and he will be angry; on some level he will resent whatever you want. She'd heard that from Mom years and years ago when she was barely big enough to go to school.

He didn't yell. Instead the big harsh voice answered her, grating.

"Hi, Nicole. You let a man sleep."

"But the bags. Please promise me you'll talk with me—you and any of your friends tomorrow about the bags that eat the ducks and rabbits in the park, and get people, maybe, too."

He didn't answer. She heard a fake snore come from him after a minute. Nicole picked her way around sleeping men and boys, headed back to the center of the room.

"Nicole," Meg said when Nicole came close. "Please don't do that again. Stay on the women's side of the room, okay?"

Maybe Meg hadn't heard what she'd said. She hoped not, and then she hoped so, because how was she going to keep the two of them safe unless she warned Meg? She looked at Meg's laptop-colored face, Meg's plump fingers dancing fast across the keyboard with the comforting clicks that told her the world had not gone crazy, that orders for food and coffee still had to be made in the proper ways and in a timely fashion. Meg hadn't heard a thing.

"I checked the NOAA on-line. The rain will be here before we can get home," Meg said. "I hope you don't mind running between raindrops."

"No," Nicole said. "Not in the least."

A perfect excuse to run the whole way. She took a deep breath.

❖ **46** ❖

Coming on dark when Dwayne drifted sideways against Meg's house, one hand on the stucco guiding him. He listened for the first bark. Useless dogs. They'd let him get this close without noticing. Too fat with treats and soft living. He could deal with them. A solid kick to the ribs, then they'd back down real fast. Dogs knew who was boss. Could smell it on you.

Meg wouldn't be expecting him. She probably saw his truck around town, but he'd kept himself away, so no one would think he had plans. Tonight he'd left his truck way over on Tarde Street. No one could say he'd been near. He noticed Officer Ray giving him the hairy eyeball these days. Who knew what lies Meg had told on him?

The window over his head had to be the kitchen window. If he could slide in a look, it should let him know who was home now at dinnertime. Best of all, if Meg were home alone, ah, he'd have a fine time then.

Fuck. Meg wasn't home. That fucking postman, Brian, sat at the table reading the paper. Couldn't be worse. Three dogs circling each other as if they couldn't decide to bite or play. What the hell was Meg doing out, with this guy in her house? Was she afraid enough to put a man watch-dog in? Not right for what he planned. Dwayne shifted back down into the bushes under the window. Suddenly it seemed both cold and damp here, his disappointment focusing the physical insults. Meg must have gone to set up the temporary warming center at the factory cafeteria.

He might go there. Meg couldn't throw him out if he acted sweet. He could get a meal, make a few points. Get in a couple digs. Hadn't seen Martin recently, but there was always Leo who was good for a bit of mischief. Maybe he could use a little help after all. Most of the guys who went to Haven were soft on her, but there were a few who didn't love Meg. Wasn't it Chicago who complained that she gave him the evil eye and accused him of stealing Ilene's cards? He had, but the way Chicago carried on you'd think he was pure as the driven snow.

Truth was Dwayne didn't want to go. Too many people in one place who all believed in Meg and her holiness. They'd vote her a saint given half a chance. A bore. No beer, no cards, and no fun.

Cold tonight. So chilly in the truck, especially after wasting all this time getting frozen and wet creeping up on the house. He wouldn't forget what Meg had done to him.

◆ 47 ◆

"Mrs. Meg. Good morning."

Meg knew who it was before she looked up. Eric, his football shoulders in-curved, loomed over her as if that meant that fewer drops would catch on his big frame. His garbage-bag raincoat glistened slick with the cold drip that had persisted into the morning.

"Take some coffee," she said. "You must be freezing."

"Not the way I'd be if I'd been on the street last night. You did well by us, Mrs. Meg. I know you have ta fight to get us in that cafeteria."

"Thanks, but I wish..."

He waved all that away with one hand while stirring six lumps into his cup of coffee.

"Where's your little Nicole friend?"

"She's at school right now. She's a friend's daughter," Meg said.

"She asked a question." Eric sipped cautiously at his hot sweet coffee, taking his time, his blue eyes studying Meg through the rising curls of steam. Meg noticed that a couple of his buddies gathered behind him, but they didn't josh with him in the usual way about how he was hogging the coffee stand and to shift out of the way so they could get theirs. Instead, she felt they all watched her, focused. Snaggle-Toothed Jimmy and Cort Chicago, Jonestown who always asked if you wanted some cherry Koolaid, and Rapper.

"What is it?" Meg said.

"She talk much to you?" Eric said.

"Some," Meg said. "She's a friend."

The men looked at each other and, as though they made a common decision, they moved back, went to joking, the kind of talk she expected. Dolores waddled up too, looking better than she had before her first treatment two days ago, but she was fading a little already. She had to make it through five more days before the next. As she explained to Meg, once they started, you were on dialysis for life. No going back, and your kidneys took their pink slip and shut down. She beamed at Meg and reached for a cup off the table.

"Hey, Old Cricket," Snaggle-Toothed Jimmy said, jerking his chin at an older man with his head shaved. "Hear you found a fortune. Show me some gold."

Old Cricket shrugged up his shoulders, shook his head at Jimmy.

"I make a fortune with my coin finder, I sure won't show you color," he said. "You'd steal it soon's I opened my hand."

An hour or so later, Old Cricket sought Meg out in the trailer.

"Mrs. Meg," he said, after tapping at the braced-open screen door.

"Yes?"

"You ever hear talk about there being pirates here in Santa Barbara, or maybe Goleta?"

"Pirates? You mean long ago? I heard about smugglers up the coast in some of those small bays, but I don't know about here."

"Well, there were, and I know it. Alien pirates because it's not wood. I found a boat. I'm going to dig it up."

He spoke fast, looked back over his shoulder.

"If I brought you something to keep for me, could you keep it? Keep it safe and keep it secret?"

"I don't usually store things for people."

"Maybe in your garage?"

That hit a sore spot, and Meg hesitated. Old Cricket pounced.

"Great. I tell you I'm on to something. Buried ship. Right in the middle of the effing Park. I'll bring it here soon as I can figure how to get it out. I think it's alien technology. That stuff is worth a fortune, and I'll donate lots to Saint Athos Church, you wait and see."

◆ 48 ◆

Brian jumped the rock in his way, half-twisted his ankle on the jutting concrete corner of sidewalk, and tore up the street toward Meg's house. He looked back once at the innocent grass, walkway, the peaceful asphalt of the street with its neat stripes of paint lying in the afternoon sun. Lying, not an accidental word, that. It was a placid, normal, palm-tree paradise landscape, with a bent-over Coke can rocking a little in the steady sea breeze that made its way through the streets of Isla Vista. The world lied to him.

He stopped to ring the bell. Brian tried to steady himself, looked down at his post bag. Top flap still down, thank God, so he hadn't scattered his mail across the park. He glanced back down the street, his ragged breath slowing. Take a deep one, slow.

"Hello, Brian. You're here early. I meant to call and ask you if you could stay here a few more nights." Meg stepped back; her hand fell to her side. She'd been reaching for the mail that he didn't have ready in his hand this time. She looked puzzled, but welcoming, less filled with energy than she'd been in the days when Dwayne lived here. He came in trying not to look urgent, closed the door behind him after one last glance away down the street. There were only apartment buildings and houses and the litter of life on a sunny day.

When Brian looked past Meg, he saw she had company.

"Nicole?" he said, surprised. "Jack?"

Nicole looked as if she hadn't been sleeping well. Peaked. Jack waved a purple can of Monster energy drink at him.

"Mom had to go out of town," Nicole said. "Dad had an accident yesterday in DC, broken leg; Mom wanted to check his diagnoses and treatments. Meg was kind enough to say I could help her move some more stuff to our place, so she'll keep me company there 'til Mom gets back. If you're willing to stay on here and watch her dogs?"

"You look worried, Brian," Meg said. "Upset?"

Takes one to know one; Brian wasn't going to say it. Besides, he was on the wrong end right now.

"Sit down," Meg said. "The kids told me they had a serious issue. Some new trouble in Isla Vista. Maybe you know about it? Seems a good idea for you to hear this too."

"Going to sound nuts, Meg and Brian," Jack said. He chugged half of his purple drink, like a cowboy in a movie taking liquid courage.

"Meg, you remember that weird thing you saw on your floor, here in the living room, some weeks ago?" Nicole said. She had her hands clenched on the back of the chair she straddled. She would switch whom she was looking at as though she were trying to give everyone in the room equal time. "The jelly animal with human eyes? You were right to feel it wasn't natural, not natural for this place anyway. It didn't belong here in your living room and it didn't come from a laboratory at the University. I have an idea that it was made, but not by people. I took a bit of the fur and skin that was left on your floor that day."

Brian felt cold on the back of his neck. He remembered running into Nicole when she'd blabbered about shopping bags and a duck. She looked steady now, but he had a perverse wish to make her stop talking, mixed with a compulsion to listen. He wrapped his icy fingers around his elbows. Shut up, stay put, and pay attention.

"I have access to my father's laboratory equipment, and I ran assays on the material I took. Amplified the genetic material. The fur was part cat. Domestic cat. The skin had masses of altered cells mixed in the skin itself, as if they'd been patch-worked, some in the fluid on the fur. These showed strange genetic profiles, not mammal, in fact, compositions unlike anything on Earth."

The way she said it you could hear the capitol "E".

Meg's face showed a fascinating puzzle of emotions. From the look of her she waited for the punch line of the joke.

"Then I saw a shape like a plastic shopping bag engulf and dissolve a duck," Nicole said. "I have an idea."

"Lots of ideas from the sound of it." Meg shook her head. "Have you thought about writing novels, Nic? I think you'd be great. You have me feeling like this is a campfire ghost story."

"I wish," Jack said. "But you've got to remember it's not fiction. I saw one of these bag creatures jelly up a ground squirrel. Thought I was crazy, or someone spiked my Monster energy drink with a recreational dose. Saw a small bird die yesterday in one of those bags. When it happens, it's fast, a matter of minutes, faster than anything I know on earth can digest something. Sometimes the bag things are dark brown or black, sometimes white or beige; they camouflage themselves to look like shopping or garbage bags."

"What logos do they prefer?" Meg asked, smiling.

"None," Jack said, as straight as possible. "I don't think they can go that far in mimicry. Some have little eyes. They move like jellyfish through the air. But we believe they are aliens masquerading as trash so we won't notice them while they predate. Disguised as a common item."

"So tell me why not a Coke can?" Meg said. You could tell she was trying to play the game and not laugh. "Or maybe a straw?"

"The bag shape allows several things—it's flexible, able to cover or enclose prey of choice. It's also mobile. If you see one blown about by the wind, you think nothing of it. If you see one moving against the wind, you assume there's some eddy or current that's responsible. The most important point is that the bags are ubiquitous. There's not a place in Isla Vista where you won't see them."

"And I've figured out another detail, though it needs verification," Nicole said. "I believe that, like any animal, these simulacrum plastic bags pass waste matter when done with their prey. That, too, has been camouflaged as another item common to our local environment. It's highly acidic in nature, and it looks like duck turds."

Brian lurched up; ricocheted by half-blind luck, he barely made it to the bathroom before he upchucked, mostly into the toilet. All he could think of was stepping into the mess on the Addison's kitchen floor, the twinkle of diamonds in the blackish sloppy material. He felt himself shake.

Now, look around, he told himself. Center yourself. Admire the tiles, the white speckled simplicity of Meg's bathroom. Follow the nice little wandering pattern of pebbles along the wall that she had the tile man put in to make it individual. Everything kept scrupulously clean until he'd come in just now. He let himself have a little time to mop up the mess and wash his hands, compulsively cleaned the fingernails with the soap bar, smelling the lilac, washed the lenses of his spectacles several times before drying them.

On his way back down the hall, he picked up his postal bag from the corner where he'd flung it.

"Here," Meg said,. She looked angrier than he'd imagined she could get. Tight-lipped with her brown eyes flashing. She handed him a cup of hot tea. Something herbal, awful, and made in the microwave instead of with properly boiling water, but he sipped it anyway, grateful for a different taste in his mouth.

"Kids," Meg said, "you are *so* out of line I can't begin to know what to say. You apologize immediately for turning poor Brian's stomach. What a way to treat a friend."

"No," Brian said. "You're right, Jack, Nicole. Both of you."

"Did you believe Jack because he's male? You didn't believe me alone, before." Nicole said.

"I didn't believe either of you in the beginning because you're kids," he said. The truth surprised him.

"Age-ism," Nicole said. "I see."

"What happened to you today?" Jack said, his long nose wrinkling as if he didn't like to ask.

"I saw one of your homeless, Old Cricket, swallowed by a bag in the bushes behind the dormitories," Brian said. Then he stopped because he wasn't sure if he'd have to run to the bathroom again.

"A man?" Meg said, her voice scaling into complete disbelief. "An entire *man*? No, Brian. This is sick. This is past a joke."

"You kids asked about his metal detector. He was using it, poking about near one of the paths to the beach. I waved at him as usual. But he froze in place, making a face—oh God, it was terrible. Agony—like he wanted to scream for help, his bad teeth all gapped. I started to jump through the bushes toward him, but he went down. This plastic stuff lunged up over him. Like a shroud. A jelly sheet. Swelling up to cover him. I could see through it while he melted into goo. His face ran, like candlewax, eyes, mouth…"

He fought his gag reflex. Swallowed again.

"I think it started after me—I felt like it could see, and there was a glitter of tiny eyes looking. I think it was too soon for it to move fast, like it was weighted down by Old Cricket, so I ran. I kept thinking I saw it, or maybe worse, maybe others at the ends of streets, and down alleys, coming to cut me off. Should I have called 911? Maybe. I didn't feel like I could. I probably shouldn't have come here, but God, I tell you we're going to need your God, Mrs. Meg, because these kids aren't lying. I don't know how many have died, I have no fucking idea how we could ever make anyone believe us. This is no 911 call."

"Film it?" Jack said into the short silence after Brian stopped.

"Great special effects," Nicole said. "I can hear it now. 'That's cool but it belongs in a movie, not a police station.'"

Meg looked at them, from one to another and then another, her disbelief palpable.

Did Meg believe them, or did she think it was some mass hallucination? Or worse yet, a joke?

"I have to go and feed Emmett," Brian said.

"Not by yourself," Nicole said. "Let's not do that stupid movie thing where each person thinks of something he or she has to do and wanders off to be axe-murdered."

"No, let's all go and get dissolved together," Brian said. "We'll write our own brand new take on how to be stupid in the land of after midnight."

"Nice title," Jack said.

"Do you mean to suggest," Meg said, her voice very quiet, "that possibly the men and women from the homeless community who disappeared recently might have been attacked? Might have died? Might be in the bellies of jelly monsters?"

The three looked at her.

"You're asking a lot of me," she said, passing her fingers up into the graying hair at her temples.

"Seems to me you're the one here with the most practice in giving a lot," Brian said.

Nicole giggled, then swallowed hard.

"Whatever we're doing, we need to do it now, before the sun sets. I don't know what sensory or mental abilities these things have, but I know I'm not as able to see after dark as when I was young, and if something's hunting me, I want to see it coming," Brian said.

"Remember they can fly." Jack tilted his energy drink one last hopeful time.

"I still don't know," Meg said. "Whatever's happening, I'm going to try and talk to the police right now. There's strength in numbers. I'll text my roommates. Make up something for them so they don't think I've lost it. Maybe they'll want to go to your house too, Nicole. But what about warning the homeless? I could text Jennifer?"

She put her hand up as if suddenly she had a headache.

"Oh God, I haven't seen or heard from Jennifer. I wonder if she's all right? Jennifer never showed yesterday to open up the Havens breakfast table and set out the coffee. Not like her to be irresponsible. She's supposed to do the first shift at the temporary shelter tonight. Maybe she stayed home sick. How will I reach everyone, spread the word? I think I better go, take her shift or see if she's come. I've got to be crazy, too. I don't even believe you, do I?"

"The cops know you, Meg, so you're the best bet to talk with them," Nicole said. "I'll go with Brian, and you, Jack, go with Meg. Rendezvous back here at Meg's."

"Yes, sir," Brian managed. He stood before squaring off to salute her. "I have my orders. I'm thinking that, with the dogs and the fact there's no fence for them at Nicole's house, maybe I hold the fort with the animal population this one night. Jack—you can pick; go home, stay at the shelter, or whatever won't freak out your parents and keeps you safe. You're welcome here. You—Meg, Nicole, and roommates, can all hold down Nicole's home. Won't scandalize anyone that way, and besides, I like dogs. They'd give warning if anything went wrong, and that way you don't need to worry about them or your house, Meg."

◆ 49 ◆

Nicole stood by the door, stroking Emmett's rough fur. Brian adjusted his backpack, lumpy with goods, handed Nicole Emmett's leash, then locked the door while she kept look-out. Oh, shit. A familiar figure came out from between the neighbor's fence and the roadway, walked up, and stopped by the peach tree.

"What have we here?"

Nicole stared at Dwayne, who stood leaning against the trunk. Big and insouciant, his mouth in a lazy poisonous grin.

"How long has this been going on?" Dwayne said. "Isn't she a little young for you, Big *Brain* the Postman? Is this why it takes so long to do your rounds? Not laziness, but the personal touch?"

Nicole kicked Brian when he started forward. Emmett growled.

"Smart dog, a lot smarter than Meggie's pair," Dwayne said. He walked backwards down the path in front of them.

"Just remember, little miss Nicole," he said, "I know who you are, where you go to school, where you live, and when your father's home. And when he's not."

A flare of mixed fear and rage dizzied Nicole, but she put a staying touch on Brian's arm. Nicole steered them down the path. She tried to project the assertiveness she'd seen her mother project. Made her feel light, oddly beautiful. She smiled a predator's tooth-baring smile.

"So sweet of you to care," she said. "I know where you hang out. I've memorized your license plate, and best of all, Dwayne Wallace, I have your fingerprints."

She kissed her fingertips to him, then turned her back at the end of the path where it led onto the sidewalk, all but dancing along.

"You bitch, you total bitch," Dwayne hissed after her, but he didn't follow them.

"Nicole, you rock like granite," Brian said. He took back the leash.

"Like granite and shale and schist," she said, then cast a wary glance about, looking for the movement of plastic, the little flutter she could so easily imagine she saw under the tire of a parked car or tucked among the bushes along the road.

"I'm sorry about Old Cricket," she said. "He always said hello. I'm having trouble believing what you saw, even though I *believe* it. Sorry."

"Yeah," Brian said. "He'd say hello, and how's about some change for an old man."

The words came out surly and hard, but Nicole looked at him, remaining silent for a few strides. Both walked fast, watchful, jumpy. Nicole double-checked something she saw, took a deep breath, then faced front.

"I wish Dwayne had moved out of town. Moved on."

"Me too. Maybe the bags will get him."

"And they'll get indigestion."

"Why did you say the bags excrete acid droppings?"

"I don't know which details are important. It's part of the data. Animals tend to get rid of what doesn't agree with them. I ran a litmus test on those droppings, and they came in low. Ranged around five. Acidic."

"Fair enough. What do humans excrete?"

"Aside from the obvious, I guess you mean in terms of PH. About seven, close to neutral. But wait, human blood is something like 7.4 PH, on the more alkaline side. Urine too? I'd assume we run slightly alkaline overall. It's depressing to think all rain is acid these days. Isn't there a condition called acidosis which is dangerous for humans?"

"Sounds familiar, but I don't know. I bet any extreme is bad for us. Never had any medical training."

"Me, neither," she said in all seriousness and didn't realize how funny that sounded until Brian chuckled, short and dry.

"You probably will, kid, if you keep on the way you've started."

"Wish I knew more. I wish I knew what's up with Dad in that hospital in DC. Mom will call when she has anything important to tell. I'm going to send them an email later."

"Hell." Brian cast another wary glance behind them, turned, switched Emmett's lead from one hand to the other, so it wouldn't tangle. "I forgot to ask. What happened? You have any idea what's wrong?"

"Accident with someone running a light. Broken leg, maybe dislocated shoulder, and he had a funny heartbeat irregularity they wanted to check out. I believe that's all. Mom doesn't believe in protecting me."

"I know you must worry, but that accident got them out of town," Brian said. "I'm thinking that's a good thing. Brings up another question. Is this plastic bag thing local? I feel like an idiot not to have thought of it before."

"I asked one of the street people a question last night," Nicole said. "I went with Meg to the temporary warming shelter at the cafeteria attached to the Rubber Protectos offices in Isla Vista last night. I wanted to talk with the folk and find out what they say, because someone said something last night that had me jumping out of my skin. Said he hoped someone *would be taken by a bag*."

"Nasty night," Brian said. "You and Meg were out late? That must have been one jumpy walk back, given what you know."

"Didn't see a thing in the drizzle."

"You think they might not like rain?"

"Not a clue." She scowled. "I didn't see any, if that counts. But plastic is unaffected by rain, so I can't think water hurts them; why would it? I've been worrying they know who I am. I don't know; I'm not certain if they *think*, if they could have some kind of hive mind. I wonder if they communicate back to a central unit, if the things we see are simple biological machines sent out to forage, directed by a mind back in the park. One thing I know is that what I've seen seems to center on Dogshit Park. Did you see all the flyers this year after Halloween about missing persons?"

"No idea if it's different from the usual," Brian said.

"It is. Normally they're looking for three or four. I asked Officer Ray and he's got his hands full trying to follow leads on a dozen youngsters who told family they knew someone in Isla Vista and planned to go to the big Halloween bash. Four or five will show up in Reno or God knows where, I hope, but how about the other seven?"

◆ 50 ◆

Meg looked up when Brian opened the door and let Nicole go skittering in before him and Emmett. Meg had Jack assembling sandwiches from the shavings she sliced off a ham bone and a loaf of homemade bread, while Meg's roommates shoveled cookies into Ziplocs, oranges and bananas into a knapsack. Looked as though Jack knew how to stack a good sandwich. The cookies smelled like they'd never seen the inside of a store, full of chips and raisins, fragrant with butter.

"We're taking our dinners to the shelter, and extras to share. I'm so sorry to change tonight's plans," Meg said. "Lincoln verified I need to take first shift. We're hitting fifty or below again tonight, possible showers, and Jennifer hasn't shown. She didn't answer her phones. Good news is, going to the shelter will give us a perfect opportunity to warn folk."

Meg's roommate Susie, took the opportunity to make eye contact with Brian. She did a circular motion with her finger around her ear, questioning. Brian shook his head solemnly. Meg whirled on Susie.

"No, I am not crazy, and Brian the postman isn't. Nor is Nicole or Jack. Ming, do you believe us?"

"Of course," Ming said.

Everyone turned to look at her with disbelief.

"I said I believe you. I'm not talking about it, but I am not staying here tonight alone. I want everyone around me in some safe place. I would rather be homeless tonight in the shelter than alone."

"I wasn't actually thinking crazy," Susie said, her voice low, gentle, even persuasive. "I was actually thinking about something like ergot poisoning. You know that wheat bacteria? In bread?"

"Fungus, not bacteria," Nicole and Jack said in chorus. Nicole continued.

"Problem is that we all have the same identical delusion, which doesn't happen with ergot."

Susie shrugged. "I'm going to finish up my studying and my work right here," she said. "I promise I will be careful, even if I think you're all delusional. Plastic bag monsters. Huh. I'm staying put."

"I'll stay here too if you don't mind," Brian said. "We'll keep the dogs with us, keep the doors locked. We'll be OK, if Susie doesn't mind my hanging around."

Susie shrugged.

"In fact, Nic and Jack, if you prefer to stay put here, you can."

"We have something to work on at the shelter," Nicole said to Jack. "I asked a question last night of one of the homeless, Eric, I think."

"Yes," Meg said. "Eric came by this morning with some of his buddies wanting to talk to you. What, Nicole?"

"I need data," she said. "Primary data about what's been happening, how local it is—all of that. I told Mom to catch Dad up on what I've been seeing. I think I'll email them whatever I find out as I get it plotted and quantified; that should keep Dad's mind off his leg and sore shoulder."

She took off her knapsack and pulled out her laptop.

"After all, who better to ask than the street people? They go all over town, they pay attention when no one else does. They must be the primary victims of what's happening. They have no shelter, except for the ones who live in cars. Brian and Susie, I promise I'll relay everything I can, even the trivia, so we can have your minds working on this, too. May not get it to you until tomorrow morning, but I will share."

"Then what?" Meg said. "We go to the police?"

That brought silence. Brian absently stroked Emmett's ears. The dog whined as though he picked up anxiety.

"Sorry, Emmett. We come up against a wall. What we need is for the cops to witness what's happening, but I wouldn't sacrifice my worst enemy to that cause, even if we could figure out how to stage it."

"I haven't even approved this split of forces. I have to get over to that shelter *now*," Meg said.

"It's not up to you," Jack said. "Free will."

"In my house?" Meg said.

"Yes," Brian said, "in your house. Even those of us who don't believe, have as much information as we can digest for now. Go, Meg, Nic; go take care of your folk. Jack, make whatever arrangements you can with your family."

"I'm going home but there's no hurry," Jack said. "Mom and Dad are at a meeting in San Diego, all they expect is a text when I'm home. But I can't go home without talking with Meg's people. I'd perish of curiosity. Can't have that on your consciences."

He shrugged, put his hands in his pockets as if declining any offer of interference.

"Any incidents in your neighborhood, Jack?"

"I was saying to Meg, no. Not that I know about. I saw a ground squirrel die in a bag. That persuaded me but it happened in Freedom Dogshit Park, not on my street."

Meg shook her coat on.

"We need to get out of here and do our jobs," she said. "Remember the front door doesn't latch unless you pull back and lean right. Don't let Popeye eat Emmett, Brian."

◆ 51 ◆

About three quarters of the way to the temporary warming shelter, Nicole looked back for the uncounted next time, and stopped.

"Meg," she said, "where's Jack?"

"Wasn't he right—"

Nicole's cell phone rang.

"Nic, it's Jack. Keep your eyes peeled. See you in fifteen. Knew you'd pitch a fit if I told you I was going a different way, so don't waste your breath."

In a fit of pique, Nicole clicked her cell phone shut without saying a word.

"Jack's okay. Idiot says he'll join us in a couple of minutes."

Nicole helped as much as she could with setting up the cafeteria. This time she had a clue what to do, stacking chairs, folding tables. She helped Meg drag a few tables into the center of the room as before. Already people gathered outside, many of them looking as jumpy about coming in as feral dogs will who aren't accustomed to having something overhead.

Nicole kept looking at the door, anxiety curdling her stomach. Where was Jack? When Meg opened up the doors, people started in, Jack with them, staggering under a load of grease-spotted paper bags, his chin clamped down over the top of his armload.

"I didn't think you had enough ham sandwiches," he said. "I've got twenty hamburgers, some with cheese, plus twenty egg-wiches. Hope any vegetarians here are ovo-friendly." He set the bags down on a table.

"I have food," Meg said, flailing between disapproval and appreciation as hungry people began to line up, sniffing the air full of that greasy, hot smell. She scrambled for words. "But none of what I have is ready yet. I would have been mixing soup from cans. This will be a treat, and if it's not enough, we can do soup, too."

Jack shucked off his bulging knapsack and started emptying the bags on the table. The guys at the hamburger joint had packed well, with two layers of cardboard box tops separating egg sandwiches from hamburgers, masses of open-topped pockets stuffed with French fries.

"At least they didn't pack it up in plastic," Nicole said.

"I asked for paper," Jack said, his hands busy. "Oh, crap. I forgot the ketchup."

"Nicole," Meg said. "Here are the keys. Go next door to the trailer. I have ketchup in the back of the office in the gray steel cupboard thing on the west side."

Nicole took off at a run out the door. She couldn't keep herself from pausing at the first corner and looking in all directions. Hardly a breeze tonight. Rain coming later, so a wind would have to rise eventually. Nothing moving when she looked around this deserted part of Isla Vista.

All the cozy coffee shops, the pho places, the tortilla havens, and the naan and curry dives were on the yuppified streets where the students hung out. This end, near the edge of the populated area where the vernal pools edged the eucalyptus rows, had no appeal for students. Not yet. Not until some developer managed to bulldoze a few more vernal pools to push the streets of Isla Vista a couple more hundred feet.

Was that motion?

She leapt up the stairs to the trailer door, then looked back. Only a gray cat, burly, with a fighter's ears, slinking from one tuft of eucalyptus duff toward a mud-encrusted Frisbee.

"Go inside, cat," Nicole called across the street before she turned to the trailer door. "It's not safe here in Isla Vista these nights. Or these days."

The sound of her own voice again made her uneasy. She glanced at the cold beauty of the sky, graceful long arms of eucalyptus trees black against the lavender and rose of building clouds. No stars tonight if the forecast storm moved in. She turned Meg's key, wrenched open the trailer door, switching on the light. Barely dark enough to need it, but she wanted to be out of there fast. There stood a gray cabinet.

She swung the steel door open spotting ketchup among other plastic bottles. Industrial size. She picked it up with both hands, curling her arm around, then settled it snugly against her hip. She slipped the keys into her pocket.

When she turned, she noticed the rest of the dingy room, blackish white sprinkled muck on the floor. What a mess. Had Mrs. Meg let ducks in here? Something wrong.... She saw it. Tan, crouching barely inside the door, a plastic bag waited between her and escape. It seemed to shift slightly in the splotty mess on the floor, as though gathering itself for a plunge.

Stupid movie idiot. She knew better, Jack knew better, Meg knew better than to send anyone out alone. One pair of eyes wasn't enough. It happened all the time in horror films. She'd been so bloody stupid to fall straight into a convention—now she was going to die here. Jack would feel terrible when he realized that she'd been killed by a convention. A trope. A fucking plastic grocery bag.

There had to be some way to hurt it. Interesting, she'd never thought about that before. The tiny row of eyes glittered at her, winking. Nicole groped behind her for some object, then glanced back. Vinegar. Big bottle of white vinegar. Big bottle of Italian dressing. Damn it. She needed a weapon, not salad makings. She grabbed the hammer on the shelf of the cupboard before she consciously recognized what it was. Then twisting back to her enemy as it lifted to float toward her, Nicole let fly. Hammer connected with bag, spinning hammer swinging the bag through the air on a new trajectory, right back out the doorway, thudding down at the foot of the steps. Nicole leapt after, kicking the door shut behind her even as some part of her internal critic groaned. *Why are you worried about someone ripping off Meg's office now while you're about to die? And let me remind you, chickie, we're talking about getting digested, alive.*

She barely paused at the top of the steps. But it took only that blink of vision to see the bag begin to pour out from under and around her hammer before she leapt way out over the steps and the bag, hitting the ground with a slam that drove most of the breath out of her lungs. Then Nicole ran. *Track*, the internal editor cackled. You made a big mistake when you didn't go out for track. She had to look back.

Nicole saw it barely off her right shoulder, effortless in its flight. No air in her lungs to scream. She swung up and back with the ketchup bottle, feeling it slip from her fingers, seeing it hit the air-borne bag to bear it back crashing to the ground, the plastic bottle splurting a tsunami of scarlet ketchup when it struck the matted earth. Nicole gasped, tasting ketchup, swiped her eyes clear, stumbling.

No ketchup tonight, guys, Nicole gulped. I used it all. *Sorry*. She leapt on two, three steps, four, fat drops of red splotting the ground around her. She raced back to the cafeteria building, thought something touched her arm, but she had nothing left to fight with, kept running, faster, not daring to look.

Funny, she'd thought the trailer was so close by, but it felt like she lived hours of running before she slammed the door closed behind her and leaned on it, sliding down to the linoleum floor inside.

"Miss Nicole, you bleeding? You all right?" Eric and some other men approached her, two of them crouching down to eye level. She didn't care that they smelled. She did, too, of vinegar, tomato, spices and sugar.

"Not blood," she managed.

"What happened? You look like you hit your head?"

"Where's the ketchup?" Meg said. She stopped when she saw Nicole. "Oh, no; Nic, are you okay?"

She gasped a few times, fish out of water, and finally caught her breath.

"I wear the ketchup," Nicole said, her voice too quiet, then tried to adjust her volume so they could hear her. "I hit one of the bags with the ketchup bottle and knocked it out of the air, I guess, because here I am, not there. Flavored up, you might say. And Meg, your trailer has duck shit on the floor."

"What?"

"Your assistant's missing," Nicole drew some more good breaths. "I don't understand. That bag should have caught up with me, those things are fast. You should have seen the ketchup hit the ground. Fountained up like blood. Maybe the bag stuck, weighed down with ketchup, because I'm here. *I'm here.*"

She made herself stop repeating it.

◆ ◆ ◆

"Slower, slow down," Jack begged, his pen scrambling across the notepad to keep up with the voices of the men. Nicole checked a box on her own pad, adding a note. She looked over at her friend in the circle of light from the desk lamp they'd moved from the office. She felt the drying ketchup itching in her scalp. Strange to be sitting here with these people, feeling safe. Mom would laugh, but Nicole knew she wouldn't be surprised. Nicole felt so much better now she'd sent her first few emails to Mom and Dad. The office was the only place in the building with internet.

"Yeah," a woman spoke, creaky, irritated. "I want a turn, too, 'cause I have things to say. These men don't know how to tell a story. For me it was a rat like you've never seen, with this big blue eye kind of like a fish eye in its side, or its shoulder, blinking at me, and a smooth pointed rat face with no mouth and nose, like a cone, a plastic cone, you know?"

"Don't see how no one could know when there's nothing like that on God's green earth," Snaggle-Toothed Jimmy said.

"Fish don't blink. You ever seen a fish blink?"

"So when's So Cal been green? God's green earth, my ass."

"Starting about a month ago, you guys have been seeing things."

"We're always seeing things, kid," a black man with Rastafarian dreadlocks said. "Depends on how bad the DTs are. Or who doused the weed with herbicide before we got to it."

"Shut up, he wants to know," Ilene said. "Besides, I never had DTs. I know what I saw. Write it down, boy."

A little after nine o'clock, Jack started to read off data from his scrawled notes while Nicole wrote on a fresh pad and Meg put in information on her keyboard. They crouched together with a motley crew of homeless men and women. About six children under the age of ten played some card game in the cafeteria corner with Lincoln that involved a lot of laughter and slapping of cards on the linoleum. Meg's face showed shadows of suppressed feeling, like bruises coming under her eyes as she finished tagging in another mark on the street map on her laptop.

"So, we're counting over twenty-some instances of seeing an animal engulfed by these things that resemble plastic bags. All kinds of the usual colors, tan and clear, white, big ones with the black or deep brown of the standard garbage bags. Right?"

"Then there are the people we think we saw killed. And the Addisons if you accept that duck shit is what the bags leave behind."

"Here," Meg said, her voice subdued. She turned her laptop so that all could see.

"Orange dots are the animals. The red dots are for the people."

"Shit," Eric said as reverently as though it were a prayer. "Isla Vista looks like measles. But Dogshit Park is scarlet fever."

Jack took a long breath, re-settled himself with his arms crossed over his knees.

"The good news is it's local," he said. He popped the tab on a new purple can of energy drink.

"The bad news is it's dense," Nicole said.

"Point of origin?" Jack said.

"Edge of the park, given that the furthest outlier episodes seem to be roughly equal from that. You triangulate and you get the south border of the park. Seaside."

"No one's been sleeping in Freedom Dogshit park for days, maybe a week," Eric said.

"Funny, that, but it's true. We share some information, warnings about when the cops are on a tear, or when the restaurants have dosed throw-outs in a dumpster with cleanser, but we hadn't more than ghost stories about this," Snag-tooth said.

"Why duck shit?" Ilene shook her head. "Why would they leave duck shit? They aren't ducks."

"We can only theorize," Nicole said, meeting Ilene's watery gaze. "But since they chose to camouflage themselves as something common in the environment, plastic bags, maybe they tried to camouflage their excretions as something else common in the environment. They started in Freedom Park, which is full of duck shit. Animals excrete compounds and chemicals that aren't good for them, so these things are animals and have a metabolism that works on the same general principles as Earth animals do. The shit is acid."

"You really calling them aliens?" Eric said. He frowned not as if he were angry or disagreeing but thoughtful. "No one ever told me about this type when I was on my spaceship."

"I sure hope they don't belong on Earth," Jack said. "I don't think anyone on Earth has the ability to perform genetic engineering like these creatures."

"Do they think?" Meg said. "Do they have souls?"

"God knows." Nicole quickly tried to cover. "I mean if God doesn't, no one does. I don't think we need to worry about whether or not they have souls right now. But if they have brains, it would explain why I thought once, they might have followed me. It would also explain why they can do genetic engineering."

"But the bags don't look brainy. If they can shift the neural connections to move their eyes, it argues no central brain," Jack said. He took a long swallow of his Monster energy drink. "What if they have a telepathic group mind centered somewhere else? Like *Wrinkle In Time?*"

"I said a neural net, and yeah, that usually doesn't make for sophisticated intelligence. I like the *Wrinkle* idea. What if they collect information for a central processor? Telepathy or radio waves or, I don't know, some kind of 'ethernet' or 'airport' connection?"

"But we need to know how to tell 'em to go home," Eric said. "I'm a peaceful man."

"These things are not nice," Ilene said. "Kill them all. Nuke 'em till they glow."

Nicole felt herself nod, caught Ilene's eye in what felt like a moment of perfect understanding.

"Easier said than done." Jack scribbled a few words down then looked up. "What do we know that they don't like? Does anyone have a clue? They seem to have eaten cats and maybe dogs, people, ducks, rats; does anyone know if they ate fish?"

"Not a clue," Rapper shrugged.

"I heard the koi place was missing some big expensive fish," Jack said.

"Oh." Charlie turned red and whispered, though that made everyone listen harder. "That was *us*. Don't tell."

"Won't," Nicole said. "So, we haven't any proof the bags ate fish. But Halloween night, when I thought they were chasing me, it started to rain. Can they have a problem with water?"

❖ 52 ❖

Dwayne had waited long enough. The night clouded over, bringing some warmth, or at least a slowing of the temperature drop. He felt itchy in his wool coat, and he wasn't hanging around twiddling his thumbs any more. Meg's car sat in her driveway with its nose under the overhang of the roof. Perfect.

He walked up just inside of the bushes that verged the driveway, pressed against the side of the house so anyone looking from the kitchen window wouldn't see him, and peered over the white painted sill. Goddamn, what was the pisser postman doing in Meg's kitchen again? Was that the man she'd settled for, once Dwayne moved beyond her reach?

Desperate for company. That little pipsqueak, his sixties ponytail hanging down his back. Would be fun to give it a yank. Probably queer. Had his own dog in there, too. Dwayne watched Brian stroke the uplifted head. Brian nodded. Dwayne saw one of the roommates. Sarah, Susie, whatever her name was. Began with a "S" sound. Brian making time with the girls?

It was dark enough now.

◆ 53◆

Something big smacked the house; the room jumped, and noise blasted Brian. He grabbed the table. The dogs froze in place, eyes white-circled. So did Susie, her face shocked in a curious gargoyle shape.

The second explosion jarred the concrete slab under his feet. He stared about, seeing a small sifting of powder scatter from a penciled crack on the wall. Incredibly distinct motes of plaster. The dogs started yelling, Popeye making a noise somewhere between a wail and a howl, the black-and-tan yelping as if Brian stepped on his tail, which, for all Brian knew, maybe he had, and little brown Emmett silent as though with shock, staring rigid at Brian. He heard everything fuzzy as though through wads of cotton. Thank God for temporary loss of hearing. At least he hoped it was temporary.

"What in hell, Emmett?" Brian said.

Susie was making human noises, he realized, when his ears began to work better. Lots of noises.

"Came from outside," Brian said, not knowing if he were talking loud enough. He looked again around Meg's warm little kitchen and went to the front door, peering out the glass window.

"Shit." Brian shoved the dogs back, got himself outside on the front lawn, facing the ball of fire that had been Meg's car. The people in the next door apartment building spilled out onto porches and front steps; he could see the characteristic poses of many telling him their cell phones were taking care of notifying the fire department, police, whoever. That second explosion had been the car's gas tank. Mostly fumes, or they'd have had a real problem.

No fire extinguisher in sight. Meg should have one, but no time for looking now. How many times had he thought Meg needed a longer hose? He sluiced the overhang of the roof. No good splashing the flammables of the little car all over the place by aiming at it, but letting the house catch fire wasn't going to happen on his watch. He soaked the garage door but again and again returned to the overhanging roof element.

Only after the white fire engines arrived did he wonder *what* had happened and why. Here came Officer Ray.

❖ 54 ❖

Dwayne heard sirens far behind him, the other side of Isla Vista. He parked his truck by the warming shelter. A little before nine o'clock, so he was in plenty of time to sign in. He shook himself off outside his truck, shucked his coat in case it smelled of burning, shrugged into his blue flannel shirt. Meg's father's blue flannel shirt. Made him grin. He took his knapsack out of the back before locking up his truck.

The evening had a cold bite to it, but clouds massed ever deeper to the south, and he thought the prediction of rain off-schedule as usual. Figured that in a place like Santa Barbara, where it ought to be simple to predict weather, the lazy so-and-sos always, in his experience, missed. They'd say rain starting by midnight, guaranteed before three P.M. everyone would be soaked. He walked up the stairs into the shelter.

"Dwayne Wallace." He gave his name to Lincoln at the door. Lincoln looked up at him, wide-eyed. Dwayne smiled, friendly, he hoped, though he wasn't sure how it came across, given Lincoln's stiff expression. *Tone down the happy, Dwayne.*

"You can't keep me out. I've a clean record, brother, and I'm damned cold."

He straightened and looked over the room full of people, the smell of unwashed people a little like the odor of old dog, with a trace of frying grease on the air. Made him hungry.

"Something for dinner?" he said to Lincoln to remind the fellow of his duties.

"We have soup and toast with cheese," Lincoln said. "You can go help yourself."

When Dwayne made his way over to the indicated table, he found himself puzzled. Things felt strange, out of order. Where were the usuals? Eric and Doug, Old Cricket and Snaggle-Toothed Jimmy? Charlie and that damned dog, Dolores, Ilene and Ginny, Jonestown with all his bad jokes about Koolaid, and that black dude you had to watch out for, Rapper. Where was Meg? He felt as if everyone he knew had left, and he was the only one who knew his shit. The five fellows already asleep didn't look familiar. Newcomers from the north come to winter in Santa Barbara. Interlopers. Other side of the room had two families or more to judge by the smallness of some of the sleeping forms. Kids in the corner with one of Meg's acolytes, playing cards.

Anxiety made him hurry on the soup, but it was hot enough. He dipped the toast with cheese into it. The next thing he expected was the police to break the news of her house burning up to Meg—that made him smile and slow down. Look relaxed. Never give a clue you have anything on your mind. She'd be around here somewhere, maybe in the kitchen.

There wasn't any evidence, he'd made sure of that. He got a second bowl of the soup. Minestrone. He's pass on the salad they'd left out; the lettuce had brown edges. Those three discount jugs of cheap Italian vinaigrette had to be more vinegar than oil.

Dwayne found himself a corner to lean against with the lent blankets and pillow. Cheap shit. Small enough pillow he almost could see slipping it into his knapsack. Not much left inside his knapsack after he'd cleaned out all the evidence into the grocery dumpster three blocks away on his way here. He burped. Of all things he missed, he missed Meg's gift with food. Out-of-a-can minestrone didn't cut it.

Nothing like a good night's work to make a man sleepy. He slipped into a drowse.

◆ 55 ◆

Brian came into the front door of the cafeteria warming center with Emmett closely leashed. He looked down at the weedy young man with a five o'clock shadow and tried to figure what to say, but Officer Ray stumping in after him didn't wait.

"Lincoln, we need to speak with Meg."

"What's wrong?"

Lincoln gestured when Officer Ray shook his head, tight-lipped, and Brian started after him toward the back of the cafeteria.

"Sir," Lincoln said after Brian. "You need to sign in."

"No," Brian said, "I'm not one of your customers. I'm Mrs. Meg's neighbor."

He could tell by Lincoln's expression that he didn't believe him, and Brian realized that with his smell of dirty smoke and sweat, smudges on his face plus the condition of his clothing, he could pass for one of the shelter people. Fortunately, Officer Ray waved at him, so Brian moved on by, feeling grateful that he hadn't had to argue the issue with the door's guardian. He unclipped Emmett, knowing the pup would stay heeled until signaled. They went through the door then into a little study crammed to the rafters with the homeless, Jack, Meg, and Nicole.

"Meg, we had an arson incident at your home this evening. Your car blew up in your driveway, totaled. Some small explosive device that ignited the gas in your tank. You owe this gentleman a vote of thanks for wetting down the front of the house or the damages would have been far more severe. I'm sorry about your car, ma'am. This is an arson investigation, so I have questions to ask you."

Mrs. Meg's hand went to her mouth. What a clichÈd gesture, but Brian put his hand on her shoulder, then pulled it back because his was one of the filthiest hands he'd seen since coming back from the Gulf. Maybe that was why he always wanted his hands clean. Hadn't thought about that before. Didn't want to. He turned to Nicole, curled up in the corner.

"What happened to you? You look like—"

"Blood? It's ketchup? Near thing—I went to get the ketchup from Meg's office in the trailer like some ditz from a serial killer movie. A bag trapped me, so I threw the bottle at it, but my fingers slipped. Great splash, I got away."

"But you made it. No burns?"

"It didn't catch me. Don't understand why, they're so fast. Maybe it ate the ketchup instead."

Her smile looked shaky. Brian felt there was something off about the story, not that Nicole lied. Five minute run from the trailer to here. He'd seen those bags move, and Nic shouldn't have made it. He grasped her shoulder and gave it a squeeze. Yeah, she was real. She also had ketchup on her shoulder, even dirtier than he was. He wiped his hand on his jeans.

Officer Ray looked back at the study crammed with people, most sitting on the floor and all studying him in varying states of curiosity and dismay as his words sank in.

"Sorry, were you having a prayer meeting in here or something?"

The scream seemed to come from no particular place, but it bounced around the room somewhere near ceiling level. A man's voice, scaled up to treble.

Officer Ray spun back on his heel, fast for a man of his bulk. Brian saw with what incredible speed his hand filled with his Glock, like magic. Ray held it out, aimed down. He scanned the cafeteria. Lines of pallets, lumps of personal belongings, scattered people. By the door a man thumped to the ground, slack as if felled by a heart attack, a billow of clear plastic surging up over his head and shoulders.

Brian, running, didn't have a clue what he was going to do when he got there. Officer Ray thrust an elbow into his belly, whooshed the breath right out of him. Brian skidded to a stop against the officer's out-flung arm, gulping for oxygen.

"Hold it," Ray said, "What in hell?"

Brian grabbed him before he could plunge forward.

"Too late. Don't touch him. Don't touch the plastic. It burns, melts things."

"God, how do I kill it?" Officer Ray stood back and raised his revolver, but what could he shoot?

Exactly as before with Old Cricket. The man's face dissolving in a wash of fluids inside the bag, now there was bone; that too eroded with incredible swiftness. Too strange to be nauseating—there wasn't any smell of decay or blood. The bag stretched to cover, thin as Saran Wrap, stretching incredibly until it held the entire man, clothes shredding then dissolving, pink of skin flushing into blood and swirling down to the meat of arms and legs. Someone made a harsh throaty noise behind him, but Brian couldn't move. Emmet growled.

"Shut the door! Shut the damned door!"

"Things coming in. Shut the door. What the hell? Is this some goddamned joke?"

A woman's shriek, sounded like Nicole.

◆ 56 ◆

Rapper stepped in front of Nicole, his big hands closing on her shoulders. All she could see was his yellow vest and red shirt.

"You're okay, baby," he said.

The homeless in the study poured out around them, faces all fixed on the spectacle at the other end of the cafeteria. Nicole saw Ilene's wide blue eyes, Eric's face grave, as if he took notes for a report to his alien friends.

"I'm no baby. I'm not okay," she said, but Rapper gave her a deft sideways shove that sent her sprawling back into the emptied study, knocking Jack down.

"Stay in there, kids. You'll be safe." Rapper snapped the door closed on them. Nicole heard the grate of the steel table outside when he dragged it against the door.

"They can't do this to us."

Jack got to his feet, nodded. They both ran at the door, bouncing off like tennis balls.

"What in hell?"

"It's the latch. I'll hold the knob turned while you hit it again," Nicole turned the knob, but it wouldn't budge. "Wait—I can't turn…"

A whispering noise, no words to it. Nicole looked around the tiny room, at the narrow window, closed against the blue night, the cottage cheese ceiling, the metal chair and ventilation grating, the cube refrigerator in the corner. The noise couldn't be the refrigerator; it wasn't running. Jack put his finger to his lips.

She thought something moved at the grating, a flicker, reflecting the ceiling light.

It extruded through. Nicole found the words in her head. Extruding pseudo-palps. Glistening like wet jelly. Like some of the simple animals—simple—my ass. It can't do that. The pulsating probes pushed further toward her, through the grating, tentative in movement. She saw them emerging on the inner side. Her side. The palps waved as though sensing the air.

The protrusions flowed back together. The bags could move through tiny spaces then. Under closed doors, through screens, through ventilation spaces.

Porifera—sponges, can do that, not complex animals. So Jack's premise was correct—this was a simple animal form, not complex, not capable of higher functions. What if...it fell into her mind intact. A bee queen equivalent, with surrogate units physically separate but controlled and commanded in some fashion she didn't know. Like the queen had soldiers under mind control. Data collected and correlated by the bee mind, the separate grocery bag creatures roaming to collect information and food, returning to feed the central brain. That would explain it all. But hell, she heard herself take a deep breath before she screamed, even at the last minute the sound hanging up in the base of her throat as though she couldn't get over the rudeness of what she did.

"Shit—they can come through screens."

"That means under doors," James said. "That means screwed."

"Safe, my ass." She had put her lungs behind it. "Get us the fuck outta here, Rapper!"

Her fingers stumbled across the face of the knob. She found the lock, twisted it with frantic haste, turned the knob. It popped free.

"Rush it, Jack." They both hit the door, banging it against the table outside, which scraped with the shriek of abused metal against the linoleum floor.

Nicole had to stop to figure out what she saw. Chaos, noise hammered them, she saw a blur of people in motion. Plastic forms slipping in the windows along the sides of the cafeteria. She saw Dwayne—what was he doing here? Gleaming black, white, and tan—billowing plastic writhed in through window cracks and under doors.

◆ 57 ◆

Dwayne got to his feet, pissed as hell. He'd been comfortable, warm, dreaming of something good—now someone spoiled it. He was going to kick some ass. He looked across the room, tried to figure who was having a seizure. That old lady? He got curious. There might be opportunity. When people had troubles, they forgot to look out. He moved around to get a better view.

What in hell? He headed toward the door but stopped. Serious shit. He'd heard something about plastic bags, maybe loaded with acid or something. Lookit that. People fell, screamed, slumped. Flapping plastic, lots of pieces, black, clear, tan. More, like they were coming in, though the door stood closed. Fuck opportunity. Too goddamn weird to stick around.

Dwayne looked around at the chaos erupting. Time to be somewhere else. He was good at that. No hero-fool here. He'd go for the closet maybe—he remembered one over at the back of the kitchen. Full of brooms or pots or something. He took a running step, saw something out of the corner of his eye, and looked back into the black wet-seal-color of a garbage bag right at eye level.

No. This couldn't happen to him. He wasn't meant for this. Someone had to save him. This wasn't his fault, he didn't deserve it. He lunged away, flinging himself as the reaching plastic lipped out, touched his wrist.

The tearing pain sent his voice screeching out in a great gust, then a scorching sensation wrapped his arms, chest; he had no air, he couldn't even groan. He heard the bag making a noise as it stretched over his chest; belly, thighs, a sort of sloppy sucking. He had to scream, fight, but no part of his body responded. Someone far away screeched high, like a girl, and Dwayne's vision narrowed down, edged in spreading black, the light smaller, smaller, until it winked to nothing.

✦ 58 ✦

Emmett whimpered then snarled by Brian's side. He looked as though he couldn't decide which of the oddly behaving people was the enemy. Hell, those bags didn't even smell like animals, no blame to the dog.

Rapper had a broom in his hands, spearing at a transparent bag that had barely freed itself from the window screen. Brian saw a kid, maybe six-years-old, throw her handful of playing cards at a flying black bag so that it fell down, too. Not for long–he saw it surge up again. He had to move. Had to do something.

Why now, why so many? Brian saw the spatter of rain against the glass of the west windows. Were the bags attacking or escap ing? Escaping rain? Had someone talked about killing these things with water? But he'd seen them in the Addisons' swimming pool before he knew what they were.

The burn of his fingertips, like acid; no, Jack and Nicole had said *a base*. A base could scorch even worse than acid. So, were these things filled with, a base compound?

Rain. The creatures went away when it rained, didn't they? Rain. What was that about rain? Acid rain. Acid shit. The body disposes of what poisons it. The pseudo-duck shit was acid. Nicole escaped the aliens by throwing the ketchup. Vinegar. The Addisons' pool guy complained the pool water was basic. Acid rain runs about 4.3.

Brian knew then, a punch of understanding like a fist to the gut, that he'd been wrong. His mouth parched with unwillingness as if it would stop him yelling.

He hadn't gone on the postal beat so he could order his own life—it was so he'd never have to order anyone else's. Never order another death. Now he must. He would.

"Vinaigrette!" He realized it was coming out of him in a scream. "Hit it with the vinegar, the dressing! It's the acid that kills them."

He lunged for the nearest plastic supersized jug—thank God it had a dispenser nozzle—aimed and squeezed; the long pungent arc of oily dressing splashed over a brown plastic bag in mid-flight. It went down like a punctured balloon and lay, panting, he would have said if he weren't so busy taking fresh aim. Holes eroded in another one he hit. He spun to let fly at one reaching for Rapper's hand. Eric had the other big bottle. Holding it out in front of him he squeezed away, and the pong of Italian Dressing filled the air. The bags fell, splatted, lurched in slowing movements, sinking into crippled splots on the linoleum. Brian ran up to cover Eric's flank, squirting dressing out in a flying arc that struck three more bags. He put his attention on the side, where bags had been invading through the window gaps, and sent another long stream of goo over them. They didn't retreat, they kept going. Eric hissed a long string of profanity, now at Brian's side as they took the invaders down.

The noise lessened, faltered, then people started talking, someone whooping with a kind of hysteric energy. That was Ilene.

Brian stared across the open cafeteria through his smeary glasses, looking for more, but now the action seemed to be over. He took a fast couple of breaths like he'd forgotten to breathe earlier. His arms ached as he slowly lowered his nearly empty jug. Nicole? Jack? Brian turned around, frantic, until he saw Jack with Nicole, holding hands at one end of the room like two lost babes in the wood.

"God help us all," Mrs. Meg said from some place behind him.

Brian put down the almost empty Italian dressing bottle and bent to pat Emmett with a shaking hand. He didn't want to deal with anything more right now than a warm dog head and the wet hot swipe of a dog tongue cleaning salad dressing from his skin.

"Who did we lose?" he said.

"Four maybe five people. No bodies, only a piece or so left, but dead, no question."

He heard a cell phone ringing, automatically put a hand to his, but it was Nicole's. She propped herself up against the wall as if she suddenly felt tired, and no wonder; sure she did. He did. They all did. Meg sat down on the floor as though someone had taken all the stuffing out of her, Jack next to her, reaching out to pull his knapsack from under the table.

"And how, Officer," he heard his own voice with surprise, it sounded so cogent, "are we going to explain this to the police?"

"Thank God you were here," Jack said.

Officer Ray shook his head, picked up a toppled chair and sat, like he needed to.

Nicole straightened, talked vigorously into her cell. She suddenly looked lots better. Brian rubbed Emmett's ears, maybe too energetically because the dog shook his head, hard. Was that a helicopter out in the distance? One of those fucking hotel copters for jumped-up Johnnies of the executive suite.

"I don't know what to say, I dunno who to say it to, but I've called in," Officer Ray said. He looked exhausted too. He hadn't even fired a shot. Brian felt inappropriate laughter swell his chest but managed to keep it down. Fired a shot. He kept seeing the spurt of dressing arcing through the air. The entire cafeteria reeked of it.

"Guys," Nicole said. "The troops have landed. Really. My Dad sent an alert to the California base specialists. You won't have to explain this to anyone—we're going to be quarantined, cleaned up, told to shut up, if I know the government, and if it's like the movies. Mom and Dad arrive tomorrow, and the men in black should be at the door now. The troops are landing."

The sound of a chopper neared, intensified. No, not one—two, or three?

"We're not getting to bed tonight," Brian bitched, but he was so happy he grinned until his mouth hurt. "You have an extra Monster energy drink on you?" he said to Jack.

"Not for you, you Coke drinker," Jack said. "Monster drinks are for the aficionados. Connoisseurs." He pulled one out of his knapsack and looked at it. "On the other hand, buddy, " he said. "Maybe you deserve it."

❖ 59 ❖

"Man, it feels good to be back home in the So Cal sun in November." Nicole's dad sat back in his rocker on the front lawn, his broken leg propped up in its cast on a plastic lawn table.

"Aren't you going to react in any way to our document?" Nicole said, pointing at the bundle of paper in her father's lap. He'd been reading it, she could tell, because it had gone from a neat stack to dog-eared in a matter of hours. Her dad rubbed his face as if it tickled.

"I don't even know where to begin," he said. "You understand all your work's going to be confiscated, too?"

Nicole shrugged. She envisioned the memory stick in her jeans pocket. Brian took a long slug from his beer. Mrs. Meg straightened in her chair.

"You're the expert, and you owe us an explanation," she said.

Dad scratched his nose, as though he thought it could buy time.

"You know I was in contact with Mom back when you, Nic, first told her about the bags?" he began.

"No—why didn't you say, Mom? I'd have felt scads better if you'd told me. I thought you thought I was crazy after all, or on drugs, because if you believed me I knew you'd tell Dad, and I thought you hadn't—"

"Shut up," Jack said. "Please. You're blathering."

"Thank you, Jack. As we speak, there's a team excavating in Freedom Park," Dad said. "They came out from the base in Arizona and the center in LA, and they'll flood out then dig up anything of interest and take the pieces away. It's out of our hands."

"I hope they're prepared for hostiles," Brian said.

"More than you know, and your tip about acid being the weapon of choice has already saved lives. God, it sounds so nutty when I say it. Vinegar, or if you prefer, acetic acid water pistols."

"You're kidding," Meg said.

"I'm picturing it," Brian said in ecstasy, "men in black with vinegar-loaded water pistols. Vinegar grenades. Vinegar repeaters…"

"Men in black dropping acid," Nicole said.

She looked about at the people sitting on the lawn, Brian under the apricot tree by Emmett, Jack with two empty, purple Monster energy drink cans and a sandwich, Meg sitting prim on a plastic lawn chair next to Mom. Nicole looked down at her own sandwich, with the cheese squeezing out, the turkey about to slip from between the double dill pickles, and realized she'd never felt so happy in her life. Sensing motion, she looked over toward the street.

Here came Rapper and Eric, Charlie and his dog tagging behind, like they weren't sure they'd been invited. Really funny looks on the men's faces, unnaturally serious. They escorted a nervous young guy in neat white shirt and khaki pants between them, and stopped when they reached the path to the front door.

The guy, freshman-in-college type, an attempt at a beard clinging to his chin, hesitated on the sidewalk. He looked at them through his black-rimmed glasses. Nicole could almost see him make up his mind, square his shoulders under the neat button-down shirt, and take a few steps towards the group before he faltered again.

Oh God, a Jehovah's Witness. Nicole felt the usual mix of apology and anger, irritation that this fellow presumed to invade her personal life contending with embarrassment for him. He brought his clipboard around between them as if he read her face and felt he needed a defense.

"We met this guy a couple streets down," Eric said. "Sounded to us like he really oughta talk to you folk."

"I'm looking for signatures to get a petition on the fall ballot," the stranger said, his voice lifting as if in a question not a statement. A memorized plea, recited to them. "We need every registered voter to support this. The chemical companies and Big

Petroleum are organizing to stop our measure from getting on the ballot. It's important. It's vital. For our environment, our futures and our lives. Would you sign here to support a ban on plastic shopping bags in California?"

About the Author

Robin Winter first wrote and illustrated a manuscript on "Chickens and their Diseases" in second grade, continuing to both write and draw, ever since. Born in Nebraska, she's lived in a variety of places: Nigeria, New Hampshire, upper New York State and now, California. She pursues a career in oil painting under the name of Robin Gowen, specializing in landscape. Her work can be viewed at Sullivan Goss Gallery in Santa Barbara or online at www.sullivan goss.com/Exhibits/RobinGowen2012.asp

Robin is married to a paleobotanist, who corrects the science in both her paintings and her stories. She's published science fiction short stories, a dystopian science fiction novel, *Future Past*, and *Night Must Wait*, a historical novel about the Nigerian Civil War.

You may contact Robin or read her blog at:
http://robinwinter.wordpress.com, or on her website:
www.robinwinter.net

www.ingramcontent.com/pod-product-compliance
Lightning Source LLC
Chambersburg PA
CBHW070934250626
47159CB00009B/3242